"Talk to me," Reid commanded.

"I don't know what to say."

"How about you tell me why you never came forward? Start there."

There was no give in his voice. None. And Ari still didn't know what to say.

"You left without saying goodbye," he continued. "Not that I want to appear needy, but when it comes to you, I *am* needy. You promised to wake me."

"I did wake you." She'd kept her promise. "You were delirious with fever. I did everything I could for you, you have to know that. I tried to help you. I did help you. What more do you want from me?"

"You left me."

"To get help. I did not abandon you. I wanted you found. I was so happy when I saw them coming for you."

His eyes blazed, caught on hers and held. A frisson of awareness snaked through her, craving his nearness, wanting his touch again, for reasons other than comfort.

Maybe this was why she'd never come forward.

She hadn't wanted to try and recreate the closeness they'd shared in the tent and not find it again.

Kelly Hunter has always had a weakness for fairy tales, fantasy worlds and losing herself in a good book. She has two children, avoids cooking and cleaning and, despite the best efforts of her family, is no sports fan. Kelly is, however, a keen gardener and has a fondness for roses. Kelly was born in Australia and has traveled extensively. Although she enjoys living and working in different parts of the world, she still calls Australia home.

Books by Kelly Hunter

Harlequin Presents

Billionaires of the Outback

Return of the Outback Billionaire

Claimed by a King

Shock Heir for the Crown Prince
Convenient Bride for the King
Untouched Queen by Royal Command
Pregnant in the King's Palace

Visit the Author Profile page
at Harlequin.com for more titles.

Kelly Hunter

CINDERELLA AND THE OUTBACK BILLIONAIRE

HARLEQUIN®
PRESENTS™

Recycling programs
for this product may
not exist in your area.

ISBN-13: 978-1-335-58448-9

Cinderella and the Outback Billionaire

Copyright © 2023 by Kelly Hunter

For questions and comments about the quality of this book,
please contact us at CustomerService@Harlequin.com.

Harlequin Enterprises ULC
22 Adelaide St. West, 41st Floor
Toronto, Ontario M5H 4E3, Canada
www.Harlequin.com

Printed in U.S.A.

CINDERELLA AND THE OUTBACK BILLIONAIRE

CHAPTER ONE

'YOU NEED TO LEAVE.'

Reid Blake looked up from the computer that had only just started receiving emails and frowned at his older brother. Impressive as Judah was—with a murderous reputation to match the fierceness of his scowl—Reid wasn't the slightest bit intimidated by the bite in his brother's words. 'Why do I have to leave? I only just got here. And I'll have you know your darling daughter invited me to stay for an afternoon tea party in a cupboard beneath the stairs. She's making cupcakes for us and everything.'

Judah's face softened at mention of his daughter and so it should. Young Piper Blake was a whip-smart laugh and a half, with the face of an angel. It was a miracle daddy Judah could ever say no to her but say no he occasionally did, and nine-year-old Pip was better for it.

She certainly didn't get sensible guidance from her indulgent uncle Reid.

Judah sighed and leaned his impressive form against the ornate wooden doorframe. Many parts of the Jeddah Creek homestead were ornate—a testament to the peerage Judah held as an English lord of the realm, even if he had grown up in Outback Australia. 'If you're not leaving now, you'd best stay the night and sling a tarp over that mosquito you call a helicopter. There's a dust storm coming in from the west.'

'Aaargh.' Reid blew out a breath and ground the heels of his hands into his eyes as he pushed his computer chair away from the desk. Internet connections out here were sketchy at best and this was his last chance to download work emails before he went altogether off grid. 'Why is it that every time I clear a few days to head up to Cooper's Crossing the weather slams down? Do the gods not think I deserve a break from the insanity? Because, believe me, I'm looking forward to the solitude.'

'Then get off the Internet and go find it,' Judah countered.

'Can't. I'm waiting on feedback on a new engine prototype I sent in at the start of the week. It's not easy being a genius with engines, a workaholic *and* a playboy billionaire bachelor. A princely catch. A stud. It's a pain in the heart, let me tell you.'

'Are you done?'

'Never knowing what a person wants from you. Your money or your love. Possibly the new solar engine prototype that's going to revolutionise commercial flight as we know it. It's an existential crisis, I'm telling you.'

His brother eyed him impassively. 'You're no playboy.'

True, but irrelevant as far as world media was concerned. 'You know this, I know this, I like to think the few women I've seriously dated over the years know this, and yet the rest of humanity has other ideas.'

'Speaking of the women you've dated—'

'Let's not.'

'Believe me, I'd rather not. But your friend Carrick Masterton phoned here the other day, trying to track you down. Something about you being best man at his wedding.'

'And I've already told him no.' Never date your best mate's sister. Reid had broken that rule half a dozen years ago in the hope that Jenna might be the one. Instead, after six months' worth of intimate conversations, travel and attention, Jenna had sold the information she'd collected on him to the press and declared herself an environmental activist. She'd declared him an intellectually stunted free market capitalist who didn't give a damn about the environment, never mind his posturing. As a footnote, she'd disparaged his sexual prowess and labelled him the most emotionally unavailable person she'd ever met. The fallout had cost him several promising business associations and one of his oldest friends. 'Jenna's in the wedding party as a bridesmaid. Apparently she's willing to let bygones be bygones.'

Judah raised a sceptical eyebrow. 'Big of her.'

'Indeed. Anything else you want to know about my personal life?'

Judah held up his hands in a sign of appeasement. 'Butting out.'

'If Carrick rings here again, tell him you're not my social secretary.'

'Already done. I was more interested in where you were at with it.'

'Obviously still petty and wounded—at least, that's how they'll spin it.' Reid let his flippant façade drop momentarily. 'There was no good hand for me to play when it came to that invitation. Carrick and his bride are getting a two-week, all-expenses-paid holiday on a barrier reef island as my wedding gift to them. My secretary sent it through a couple of days ago. I suspect that's why he called here.' It would be interesting to see if Carrick ever took that trip, cashed it in, or ignored the gift altogether because he thought Reid was insulting him.

'You're sending him to *our* island?'

'Of course not. There'd be pictures of the

beach house splashed across the Internet within moments of their arrival. Carrick's fiancée is a social media influencer.'

'Joy,' Judah murmured dryly.

'I booked them some kind of high-end honeymoon island we have nothing to do with. They'll love it—should they choose to go.'

'Fair.'

'Keep an eye out for a headline exposing my unconscionable largess, my callous insensitivity, or both.'

Judah nodded. 'I'll have it framed and sent straight to the pool room.'

This raised a smile, as it was likely meant to do. 'Thing is, I do wish my old school mate a strong, nurturing, *happy* marriage. I want that for him. Hell, I want that for *me*.'

It was the closest he'd come in years to admitting his loneliness.

Judah sighed and wrapped a big hand around the back of his neck, a sure tell that he was uncomfortable with the turn the conversation had taken. 'You staying or going?'

'Going.' Right after he looked at the weather radar. Or maybe not, given how long it would take for that information to download. 'Going right now. Just as soon as I collect my cupcakes and say goodbye to your women. You realise they like me better than they like you?'

'If I truly believed that I'd have to shoot you.'

'You *say* that…but would you do it? Would you really?'

Judah smirked, cutting creases in his weather-worn face. 'They do say practice makes perfect.'

It was a testament to how solid their relationship was these days that they could talk freely about the incident that had put Judah in prison for most of his twenties. On the other hand, Reid had his own suspicions about what had gone down on the night of that shooting and, no matter how many times he'd tried to get Judah to reveal all, his older brother had never confided in him. When he was younger, that lack of trust had worn Reid down like sandpaper on sapwood. These days, Reid had a far more flexible understanding of what people 'needed to know'.

'Dust storm incoming,' Judah said again. 'Didn't you say you were leaving?'

He was. He couldn't wait around for a weather map that might never download. Besides, wasn't as if he wouldn't be able to see a dust storm coming. 'See you in a week.'

'The homestead's all stocked up and ready for you.'

'Aw, you shouldn't have.'

'I didn't. Gert swung past last week.'

Gert had been Jeddah Creek station's part-time housekeeper ever since Reid could remember.

She served two other remote Outback stations as well, driving a circuit around the three properties every two weeks. When Reid and Judah had bought the Cooper place to the north it had seemed only smart to keep that rotation in place for as long as Gert wanted the work.

'Fly safe.'

Reid nodded as he shoved his laptop and cord connections into his carryall and zipped it closed. He'd been flying helicopters since his teens and designing and building them since his early twenties. That 'mosquito' outside had a revolutionary engine design and a flight range more than double its closest competitor. 'I always do.'

Twenty minutes later, after a quick safety check and two cupcakes, Reid was in the air and heading north. There were no other passengers—he was on his own at last and happier than he'd been in a long while.

Judah was the reclusive rebel of the two Blake brothers, which meant that Reid often doubled down when it came to fronting the various company holdings they held between them. Reid was the people person, the gregarious showman everyone could talk to without fear. No one—and that included his brother—knew how much he hated the constant scrutiny he was under twenty-four hours of every day, or how the flippant, indestructible, playboy veneer he'd cultivated over the years was beginning to seem like a bad idea. Mainly because after years of shielding his innermost feelings from absolutely everyone, he no longer knew how to let people in.

Every move one of his engineering companies made was scrutinised by the market, by other companies on the cutting edge of renewable energy, and by an ever-increasing array of lobby groups. Markets rose and fell beneath the weight of his words. It was enough to make him wish for the good old days when it was just him, alone at seventeen, with only a vast and fickle channel country cattle station to care for.

His parents recently deceased and his brother in prison for killing a man.

Yeah, the good old days.

There'd been no functional adults in the room when his brother had got out of jail and together he and Judah had bought up vast tracts of Australian channel country and set about turning it into a reserve. No one to stop Reid as he'd poured money into renewable energy research and prototype engines geared towards clean energy flight. No one to warn them that vast amounts of money, power and position attracted even more money, power, position and responsibility, ready or not. And they *had* proved ready. Reid was proud of everything he and Judah continued to achieve.

But some days, and this was one of them, all he really wanted was blue sky all around him and the red dirt and saltbush scrub of channel country far below. After months of relentless hard graft—be it intellectual, social or political—and way too many people urging him to go faster, slower, sideways or over a cliff, there truly was no place like home.

He pointed the little helicopter north over familiar ground, his attention split between the harsh beauty all around him and the faint hint of dust in the sky to the west. Dust storms weren't that uncommon but flying into one was not recommended. Even the air currents ahead of a dust front were dangerous. If he had to land and let the weather front roll over him he would, but it wasn't his first preference.

Outrunning it was by far his preferred plan.

'C'mon, little darling, gimme all you got.' He maxed out the speed and felt a familiar sense of exhilaration slam through him. He'd been a lonely teen out here after his father had died and before Judah had been released from prison. Flying had been his first love and it still ranked right up there with sex as far as he was concerned.

Not that he'd ever mentioned it. The ridicule potential attached to his preference for flight above sex was high. He'd never live it down.

Billionaire Stud. The media ate that one up and

people believed it, and for all that Reid joked his way around it, and used it as a shield to hide a tender heart, the description grated. Even before his disastrous experience with Jenna, he hadn't been able to tell if a woman wanted to get up close and personal with him because she actually liked him. Too many women over the years *had* wanted him for his money. That or they'd wanted him to use his influence to forward their political agendas. They'd used him to advance their careers or, like Jenna, claim a spotlight they couldn't command on their own.

Romantic relationships had been so transactional for so damn long...

Was it any wonder he preferred flying to sexual intimacy?

That wall of dust—and it *was* a wall, stretching to the north as far as the eye could see—was edging closer. 'Sweetheart—' he patted the console in front of him '—we need to go a little faster.'

Ari Cohen looked behind her at the wall of rapidly approaching dust and scowled. It had come up out of nowhere and was heading straight for her, and that meant breaking camp and getting as much of her stuff into the cabin of her battered old ute as fast as she could. Once that was done, she needed to find rocks to choc around the tyres and after that it wouldn't hurt to tie the vehicle down using rope and metre-long steel fence stakes hammered into the sandy ground as far as they would go. Only then would she feel safe while riding out the storm from inside the cabin of her ute.

She'd weathered dust storms before, ever since she was a kid, but she'd never seen a red wall of doom like this one before. A snappy wind whipped at her chestnut-coloured hair and blew the edges of her tent into the air as she collapsed it and quickly rolled it up, poles and all, and shoved it into the back seat of the twin cab. Her little gas cooking burner went in next as she grumbled about the 'too little, too late' nature of weather forecasts in general and the undisputed fact that no one really cared what kind of weather events happened out here in the middle of nowhere.

Not as if anyone actually *lived* out here except for the super-rich Blake brothers, who likely owned big chunks of Mars as well by now.

Ari was throwing tie-down ropes over her ute when first she saw the silver and black blob in the sky that turned out to be what looked like a muster helicopter—a tiny thing with a bulbous nose and slender rotors and next to no seating room.

If whoever was flying that thing thought they had any chance at all of outrunning the dust roiling towards them at what felt like a million miles an hour, they were sadly mistaken.

'Land, you maniac!' she yelled even though they'd never hear her. It felt good to say it. No one could ever say she hadn't told them.

Her heart caught in her chest as the helicopter lifted straight up and then arced to the right, as if flung about by the hand of capricious winds. She didn't want to be witness to tragedy. All she wanted to do was crawl inside the safety of her vehicle and ride out the storm as best she could, but she couldn't look away from the fight in the sky—helicopter against the elements, and how was man supposed to win against those odds? What fool thought they could? 'Come down!'

It was as if someone had heard her wish, because the little aircraft spun, tilted and headed for earth and— Oh, no.

'Not like that!'

No! Oh, hell no!

So much for rocks under wheels and big load tie-downs. When that little buzz box landed, it was going to land *hard*, and there was no one else around but her to go and see what—if anything—could be rescued.

She wasn't a doctor, nurse or medic of any kind. She'd never belonged to the SES or the military.

Driving towards disaster was so not her thing. But...

And why was there always a *but*?

She'd been born and bred out here on the edge of the desert and she *knew* what happened out here when there was no help on hand. This wasn't a forgiving land.

And whoever was in that blasted helicopter was going to need a hand.

She could curse with the best of them, and let loose as she started the engine. Who was to say her ute wouldn't be picked up and slammed down by wind that had slipped its leash? But she gunned the engine anyway and set out north, her hands loose around the steering wheel on account of the soft dirt that would send wheels one way or another, no point trying to resist that sway.

She could still see the way ahead. Still see the helicopter battling capricious winds. Not down yet but getting ever lower in the sky.

'Fight,' she willed whoever was up there flying that thing.

Win.

For all his years of flying, Reid had never known weather like this. Any sense of superiority or confidence bestowed on him by humankind had long since left his brain. Getting the small craft on the ground was all that mattered now. Dying had to be factored into calculations. The efficiency of engines mattered nothing in the face of nature's reckoning.

He'd long since lost sight of the ground. None of his instruments worked.

He didn't know which way was up, and helicopters couldn't glide towards the ground and count on gravity to be their friend. Helicopters were the buzzy bees, the frantic winged. When something went wrong they plummeted.

And still he fought. Tried to feel which way was up, which way was down so he could edge ever lower. Easy. Easy, sweetie, as he fought the air and the dust that flung them this way and that with careless abandon.

This couldn't be the end.

It couldn't.

If he lived, he would definitely prioritise sex over flying. Make a solemn effort to give it all he had. *'I promise.'*

If he lived…

It was a miracle Ari even found the crash site, given the red dust blasting what was left of the paint from her vehicle. Never again would she screw up her nose at miracles, because there it was in front of her, the little helicopter of many scattered pieces, nose down and tail up and its rotors heaven only knew where. There was no one *in* the wrecked remains. No one she could see.

Where might a person land if they'd been flung somewhere?

Ari had no idea.

She cut the engine on her ute that might never start again after driving through this hellscape, but that was a problem for later. She had dust-free air here inside the cab, safe haven.

She could die out there.

Someone else *was* out there and whether they were already dead was anyone's guess, but, if they *were* still alive, they wouldn't last long unless they took shelter. That or someone *got* them to shelter. Meaning her.

What a thought.

She took a nylon strap meant for securing cargo rather than people and wrapped one end around her waist. She put her sunglasses on and wrapped a scarf around her head and mourned the lack of scuba-diving goggles because she could have used them too. Ari left the safety of the ute, hunched against the wind and the bite of dust against the bare skin of her ankles and hands. She tied the other end of the cord around her waist to the bull bar. The cord extended thirty metres at most and if she couldn't find anyone before that nylon stretched taut, she'd try again from a different direction.

'Fight,' she muttered from beneath the scarf now plastered to her head. 'I can *feel* you.' She truly could, another miracle, no matter the how or the why. 'I'm goddamn *coming* for you. Don't you give up on me now.'

CHAPTER TWO

HE COULD BREATHE. The sound of fabric snapped all around him and he couldn't see a thing, but he could breathe and he wasn't alone.

'Who's there?' His voice sounded thick to his ears and the pain in his head threatened to drag him under, but he got the words out somehow.

'He speaks.' That voice held a faint edge of hysteria, but he'd never been so grateful for the company. 'Listen.' Her voice held compelling urgency. 'Was there anyone else in the helicopter with you?'

'No.'

The woman exhaled noisily. 'That's good. That's real good.'

'Where are we?' He still couldn't make his tongue work.

'In a tent next to your crashed helicopter. I didn't know if it was a good idea to move you so I brought the tent to you. There's a dust storm. It's bad in here but it's worse out there.'

'I can't see.'

'It's dark. It's the dust.'

'No. I can't *see*.'

Silence.

'Say something!' he demanded, reaching out towards the voice and clutching onto warm skin. An arm above the elbow, bare dusty skin, warm and alive. 'I can't see.' He felt a hand thread through his, calming him, grounding him.

'Pretty sure you hit your head,' she offered quietly.

Talk about stating the obvious. But he wasn't alone and he was still breathing and maybe he should start being grateful for small mercies. 'You'll stay?' It was vitally important that the pretty, panicked voice didn't go away.

'Yeah. Not going anywhere right now. It's brutal out there.'

'I can't see.' The blackness, the sheer *absence*, overwhelmed him.

'I hear you.' She brought his hand to her lips, their fingers still entwined, and her lips felt pillow soft and warm against his skin and he focussed on that above all else. 'I've found you.' And almost in a whisper, 'I just can't help you.'

He was clocking out again, consciousness fading beneath the agonising pain of…everything. 'Stay.' He was begging, and he knew it was a lot to ask but he didn't want to die alone.

'I don't think you're dying. Your pulse is pretty strong, yeah.' Raggedy raspy sandpaper voice chock full of dirt but so beautiful. Was she a mind-reader? How did she know his thoughts?

'You're talking out loud,' she said next, dry as dust, and he laughed, or tried to, but darkness ate at his consciousness moments later and he realised that any laughter, any movement, was a really bad idea.

'I'm not… I can't…'

'You're talking and you're alive,' she murmured. 'We can work with that.'

He squeezed her hand and she squeezed back. Right before the darkness took him.

When Reid next came to consciousness, he wasn't alone and for that he was grateful. His saviour had tucked in beside him, a warm presence and a soft breath against his shoulder, her fingers loosely folded over his wrist as if she'd fallen prey to slumber while checking his pulse. The tent—she'd said she'd put a tent up around them—no longer strained against a brutal wind but there was still a heaviness in the air and an unnatural silence all about them.

He could wiggle his toes and move his legs. His fingers moved and so did his arms. He could think. He could breathe.

He still couldn't see.

'How long's it been?' Might as well ask. The body next to his had tensed as he'd run through his body check. He knew she was awake.

'A while.'

'Doesn't sound as windy.' The tent no longer shuddered beneath the onslaught.

'I think it's because the tent's half buried beneath the dirt. The weight's pressing in on my body. You got the good side.'

She moved. Levered herself up on her elbow, he imagined, because the rest of her was still pressed against him. He tried to imagine what she looked like and came up empty. He had no idea.

Was she married? He wanted to fold her hand in his again, bring it close across his chest and search for rings. 'Will anyone mind if I never let your hand go?'

'I'll mind, at some point. But no one else is likely to mind.'

'How old are you?'

'Twenty-three.'

'Are you pretty?'

'Does it matter?' she chided.

'That a no?'

'Handsome, you are stuck with me in a tent in the middle of a desert in the middle of a dust storm and I'm just about to bring you food and water *and you can't see me.* Do you really give a damn what I look like?'

Well, when she put it like that... 'I'm Reid,' he said.

'I know who you are.' She let go of his wrist and moved away.

'No, wait!' Panic set in, fierce and overwhelming. He flailed for purchase, grabby hands that would have grabbed but for the stabbing pain in his head. That keening sound in his ears? It was him.

'I'm coming back.' She put her hand to his chest and pressed down as if she knew his heart needed holding in place. 'My ute's not far away and even if I can't see it for dust, I'm tied to it. I'll get there.' She fumbled with his hand and pressed it to her body. He could feel the knotted nylon around her waist. 'All I have to do is follow the line.'

'How will you get back?'

'I found you, didn't I? Went back for the tent, found you again and put the tent up around you after cutting the floor of it in half and tucking it around you. And if you believe that was fun or easy, I have a harbour bridge to sell you. I also have pain-relief tablets back in my ute. A few types. Does that sound good? Worth a round trip?'

'Get them,' he urged. 'Give them.'

'Let go of my hand.'

Now there was a problem. No way was he letting go of that hand, and he told her so using language his dear departed mother wouldn't have approved of. In his defence, he was probably going to be reunited with his mother sooner rather than later and he could apologise then. 'Stay.'

'Seriously?'

Manhood be damned, he wasn't letting her go. ''S dangerous out there. You shouldn't go.'

'What about the painkillers?'

'Who needs 'em?'

'I'm thinking you do.'

Maybe that was true. 'How come you're here?' This was nowhere land. People didn't live here. People didn't travel through here. 'Are you real?'

'I'm trespassing. Trespassing, unmarried, and not pretty in any standard sense of the word. My eyes are too far apart, my neck is too long, my nose has a bump in it from when I broke it as a kid and I'm skinny. I'm not that clever and most times I come across as too shy to bother with. But I am real.'

'Good. That sounds good.'

She laughed and it was the loveliest sound in the world. 'See? You're almost making sense—that's a good sign. You're following the conversation, your pulse is strong, your breathing's not rattly. I'm no medic but those are good signs. You're a tough guy.'

'That's me.' A great wave began to wash over him from the toes up, thick, visceral and dragging him under. Again.

'Reid? Reid!'

He couldn't hold on.

Not even to her hand.

Ari unzipped the tent flap and squirmed through the exit before zipping it back up from the outside. Concern for the wounded man had overridden her desire to stay inside the tent. She'd already lost her scarf to him when she'd wound it around his head to try and stop the bleeding, but she could lift her T-shirt up and put it across her nose and mouth so she didn't cop a lungful of dust, and she had a first-aid kit in the ute, and a pack of painkillers in the glove box, and enough water to see them through for days.

Please let his rescue not take days.

The man was a billionaire last she'd heard. Surely, he'd have tracking devices all over that little helicopter or amongst his personal belongings.

They'd know where he was and soon as the dust cleared they'd come for him.

The dust was still so thick! He wasn't the only one whose eyes weren't working properly.

Pulling the T-shirt all the way up over her head, she took hold of the rope with both hands and pulled it taut and began to walk. She kept the rope tense and shuffled along and made it to her ute an eon later.

But her trusty old ride was right where she'd left it, even if it was now buried up to its axels.

She tried to shake the dust off before she got into the cabin, a stupid move if ever there was one, and finally settled for clambering in regardless and slamming the door shut behind her.

Better, much better as she brushed the dust from her face and tentatively opened her eyes, blinking hard. Grit everywhere. Up her nose. In her mouth.

Don't rub your eyes, Ari.

When instinct demanded she do just that. Don't move for a bit. Just…let the dust settle. She leaned back with her head against the headrest and slowly wiped at her face with the edge of the hand towel she kept just behind the front seat. It felt blissfully free of grit and she reached for the water bottle in the centre console next and unscrewed the cap with her eyes still closed and brought the bottle to her lips. Not cold, but very definitely wet.

She wet the edge of the towel and gently dripped some into her eyes until she could open them without feeling as if her eyelids were scouring pads. See? Easy as pie getting from the downed man back to her vehicle. She could do this all day.

Although it'd be nice to only have to do it once.

No phone service out here but she checked the phone's remaining battery and then set about filling her backpack and another carryall with supplies. If she was quick enough, she might be able to retrace her footsteps before the wind blew them away. She shoved her native plant identification book in the pack too—as a reminder of a wider world full of research and technology and all sorts of clever people. People who would come for the unconscious billionaire and make him well.

Until then, he had Ari, queen of nothing special, and she'd do her best to make him comfortable.

The trek back took longer because she lost track of her footsteps and the wind blew up again and so did the dust, and this time she couldn't keep her eyes closed and rely on the rope to take her where she was going. By the time she found the tent she'd begun making bargains with whoever might be listening.

If you show me the tent, I'll stop swearing for a year.

If you stop with the dust, I'll study my heart

*out and top my horticulture course in every sub-
ject. Yes, even soil physics.*

*If he lives, I'll be grateful for ever that I don't
have him on my conscience for the rest of my
days. That's got to be worth a pledge to abstain
from sex for at least a—*

Oh! The tent. Hooray!

Right in the nick of time.

'I'm back,' she said as she dumped her bags at
the door and went around to her side of the tent
and began scooping the fine red sand away from
it with both hands. 'Are you awake?'

He groaned. Still in the land of the living.

'Awesome.'

Under other circumstances she wouldn't have
minded seeing that handsome devil flat on his
back and groaning just for her, but this was not
that fantasy. She dug faster, wanting a little less
weight on her side of the tent so that once inside
there would be more room. For all that the tent
was supposed to be a two-man job, Reid Blake
had done his damnedest to fill it all by himself
and the likelihood of them both having to shelter
in it for the foreseeable future was high.

'Can you see anything yet?' Because she was
of a mind to strip off most of her clothes before
going inside, seeing as they were caked in dust.

'No.'

Not so awesome for him.

By the time everything but her clothes was in the tent, she'd broken her promise to not swear for a year.

Reid had somehow dislodged the bandage from his head and had likely been prodding at it with his fingers and then he'd used his fingers to examine his eyes. Either that or he'd started bleeding *from* his eyes. Either way, hello the stuff of nightmares.

'What is it? What's wrong?'

Did he sound sleepy or slurry and did it even matter, what with all the blood loss?

Don't panic, don't panic, don't panic, aaargh!

She was panicking.

She wondered if he could sense it.

'Nothing's wrong.' She tried to keep the fear out of her voice and failed miserably. What would she want from a protector she couldn't see? Reassurance of normality. Something to cling to. Humanity. The ridiculous nature of existence, even. 'Well, nothing except for the part where the dust is worse than ever so I left my clothes at the door and I'm really hoping you can't see me because that would be awkward.' She dragged her backpack closer and unzipped it, spilling everything onto the ground, including her torch. He wasn't the only one who could barely see in this weird twilight world of dust and—

'You're…naked?'

'Almost,' she replied as she pointed the torch at the wall and turned it on. Great. Now she could really see the mess he'd made of himself and it was even more terrifying beneath the bright LEDs. He had no colour to his skin other than blood. His left trouser leg was soaked with it. 'Almost naked, yeah. Better still, I have painkillers. They're capsules so you'll have to swallow, but I have water here too. *Can* you swallow?'

He showed her rather than told her and she sent up a silent cheer as she dragged a sleeveless cotton sundress over her head. 'Okay, here comes the first tablet. You're getting three, with a sip of water after each, and then I'm going to clean up your face and do stuff to your leg.'

'What kind of stuff?'

'Good, lifesaving stuff.'

'And you're going to do this naked?'

'That's the way I roll, although I did just pull a dress over my head. But you...what a guy. Half dead and still with the sexy thoughts. I'm impressed.' She really didn't want to examine her own response to the wounded man she tended. What kind of woman came across a man in grave danger and thought to herself, *I bet skin-on-skin with you would be a glorious thing to experience*? She tapped the first tablet against lips that were softer than they looked, and warmer too, and that was a good thing from a first-aid perspective, even if the small contact sent a tingle of sexual awareness through her. 'Not going there.'

'Going where?'

'Straight to hell, most likely. Take your medicine. Don't make me shove it down your throat, because I will. Have you ever given a cat a worm tablet?'

He laughed weakly, and she caught a glimpse of teeth, a hint of tongue against her fingers and then the capsule was gone. She barely refrained from stroking him as she would an obedient moggy. 'I don't want to lift your head up, so get that capsule to the back of your mouth and I'll pour some water into your mouth and try not to drown you, and then you can swallow. Is that a good plan?'

It was her only plan and she hoped it had legs. Imagine trying to explain to a coroner her part in this man's death. Yes, your doctor, sir. He drowned in the middle of a dust storm in the desert. Lungs full of water. I've no idea how that happened... 'Are you ready?' She dribbled water into his mouth and waited way too many seconds until he swallowed. 'Did it work?'

'Yes.'

Twice more, he swallowed the pills, and then she ripped the wrapping from a bar of milk chocolate and took a big bite. This was *her* medication. Food for her frightened soul. 'Want some?'

'What is it?'

'Chocolate. I hear it chases away bad thoughts.'

His lips quirked upwards. 'Where'd you hear that?'

'I read it in a book. Possibly a book about wizards.'

'I'd laugh but laughing sends me unconscious.'

'Do you want some or not?'

'Yes.'

She broke off a square and fed it to him by hand. She had to stay snarky if only to balance the tentative tenderness of her touch. 'Your leg's bleeding. I'm going to take your trousers off.'

'Now you're just having a lend.'

If only. 'Yep, that's me. Injured man at my mercy and all I want is a look at his equipment.'

He paused as if listening to something she couldn't hear. 'Is it really that bad?' he asked, his lovely baritone little more than a rumble.

'It looks bad from the outside,' she admitted. 'But I have bandages and stuff.'

'Stuff.'

'All the good stuff. Please may I take off your trousers?'

'Stuff of my dreams.'

She laughed. Too high, all wrong, but his lips tilted up again.

'Now that's a nice sound.'

His words steadied her. She wouldn't panic

if he didn't, and he seemed determined not to. If flirting got them through this without falling apart, surely she could embrace it? Chalk up this strangely intimate connection they were forging to extraordinary circumstances and keep doing whatever it was they were doing. She reached for the clasp on his jeans. Button-ups, all the way. Fancy pants, with plenty of weight to be going on with as she clenched denim in her fists and tugged them down his hips. 'We should try this again when you're feeling better.'

'We should.'

But his voice sounded thin and by the time she had his jeans off completely he was gone again, saying hello to oblivion.

She had gin in her carryall, don't judge, and she used it to clean up his leg before bandaging it tight. There had been no spouting artery fountain, just a deep seeping cut across thigh muscle, and she hoped her cleaning was thorough enough and that her fix would hold until proper medical care arrived.

She took care with his face. A bottle of water and her trusty towel removing the blood until she found the seeping gashes slicing up his forehead. She flooded the surgical gauze in the first-aid kit with alcohol and pressed it to the wound, and then picked up the long roll of stretchy bandage and slid her fingers beneath his head and bandaged it tight. There would be no prying this one loose. She'd smack him if he tried.

She tended to his other injuries next and tried to make sure he wasn't bleeding heavily from any other body parts.

He roused a little towards the end. 'How's your serenity?' he muttered.

'I'm predicting you'll live.'

'That's just hope.'

'I'm willing to embrace it.' She gave him more water. 'And now we wait.'

'Are you still naked?'

'Nope. I'm wearing a dress.'

'What colour is it?'

'Green.'

'What colour's your hair?'

'Dark brown.'

'And your eyes?'

'Also brown.'

'I'm picturing that actress from one of the James Bond films.'

'You do you, sunshine.' Who knew which actress he meant? She sure didn't. 'Where were you flying to?'

'North of Cooper's Crossing homestead. There are a couple of eco lodges up there.'

He really did seem functional in the thought department. 'Anyone expecting you?'

'No. The place is empty.'

'Will anyone be tracking your flight?'

Silence.

'But your helicopter has signals and stuff, right? An indestructible black box?'

'It's not a commercial passenger jet, angel. It's a prototype.'

'That's just disappointing.' She tried to let the reality of no one being able to find them using some kind of beacon sink in. 'Mind you, no one's coming for us in this weather anyway. How are you feeling? Is the pain medication kicking in?'

'Not even close.'

'It's not as if I can keep giving you more.'

'I know.'

She felt so useless. 'More water?'

'Please.'

One more pill couldn't hurt, surely. She fished one from the bottle and pressed it against his lips. 'It's just over-the-counter paracetamol. The first three were NSAIDs. I think I can give you both, but no more for another four hours after this one. You in?'

He was.

'How's the eyesight?'

'Frighteningly absent.'

She couldn't imagine a world of perpetual darkness.

'Keep talking,' he said gruffly. 'Please.'

She bit off another mouthful of chocolate,

reached into her carryall for her textbook and stretched out next to him on her stomach, making sure they were connected from shoulder to toe as she spread her sleeping bag over them both. It wasn't cold yet but it would be later. Might as well get a head start on the warm and cosy factor.

She opened the book up to a random page and cleared her throat. 'Sturt's Desert Pea, Swainsona formosa. Family, Fabaceae. Named after the English medical doctor and botanist Isaac Swainson—he'd probably be pretty useful right about now. Formosa from the Latin for beautiful. I've never seen them this far north. It flowers from March to July but that's rain dependent. It prefers calcareous sandy soils. Calcareous—what does that even mean?'

'Who are you?' he murmured.

'I'm your dust-storm buddy.' She kept on reading aloud, one plant classification and description after another, while his body relaxed against hers and his breathing became slow and regular.

Gotta give it to her textbook—it *was* useful. She'd never again rant about the astronomical cost of it.

Because it had put sightless, seriously injured billionaire Reid Blake firmly to sleep.

CHAPTER THREE

WAKING FELT LIKE rising through mud. So much mud weighing Reid down, wanting him to stay in that place where pain couldn't reach him and fear couldn't overwhelm. But fear had a way of tunnelling, and it roused him just enough to become aware of the stabbing pain in his head and an all-encompassing darkness. 'I can't see.'

He heard movement beside him and felt warm fingers circle his wrist. 'Do you know where you are?'

'I—' No.

'You're in a tent in a dust storm,' the sweet voice continued. 'Your helicopter crashed. You have a head wound and more.'

It was the voice from his dream. Or maybe it wasn't a dream after all. 'You were here before.'

'I found you. Put a tent up around you and gave you some painkillers.' He felt the press of a drink bottle to his lips and drank gratefully and ignored the trickle of water that escaped from the corner of his mouth and etched rivulets down his neck. 'Sunset was a couple of hours ago.'

He felt movement beside him and then the hand was gone from around his wrist. 'Put it back!'

'What?'

'The hand. Put it back! *Put it back!* Anywhere, it doesn't matter. Please.'

He now knew what startled silence sounded like. And then a warm, small hand pressed gently on his shoulder and he could breathe properly again. That touch, human connection at its most basic—it anchored him.

'Do you want my knees digging into your side too?' She sounded a little shaky—nice to know he had company in that regard. 'Because I want to sit up to check you over again, but if I do that, I'm gonna be all up in your space.'

'Dig in. Please.'

'You rich guys. So kinky.'

'You know who I am?'

'Yeah.' The hand stilled. 'Do *you* know who you are?'

'I haven't lost my mind.' Just his sight.

'Just checking. Far as I can tell, the bandage has stopped most of the bleeding from your head. I used up the rest of the bandages on you too, while you were out to it. There's one around your other wrist and hand—pretty sure you have a break there, and your shoulder looks out of place too. And I hope you didn't like those trousers too much, because I sliced them straight up the legs so I could stop the bleeding from the gash that runs from mid-thigh to your kneecap. And then I unbuttoned your shirt to check out your abs. Looking good, by the way. Then I slid my hand underneath you and groped all over your back and your butt—'

'Who's the kinky one now?' he murmured.

'And when my hand didn't resurface covered in blood, I decided you probably weren't bleeding out. After that, I kinda just tucked in beside you to wait. I figure your big brother will be trying to find you soon, but he's going to have to wait for the dust to settle first.'

'You know Judah?'

'I know of him. Same way I know of you. Hard not to around here.'

'So, you're local?' Was she being evasive with her identity or was he imagining things? 'I'm not about to sue you for trespassing, if that's what you're worried about.'

'Funny guy.' She patted his shoulder. 'I don't have any money for you to get and I doubt you'd want my ute. It's a relic held together with duct tape and baling twine and have you seen the cost of diesel these days?'

'So you're a broke horticulture student on an

Outback camping trip?' Their earlier conversation was starting to come back to him. That blasted plant book.

'Sounds about right. I had a job mowing lawns and trimming hedges in Brisbane. Cleaning garden goldfish ponds and water features, keeping permaculture closed water systems in shape—I really liked that part of the job, but then my boss had a heart attack and sold the business and the new owners were a young husband and wife couple and there wasn't enough work to keep me on.' She sighed heavily. 'I have three thousand dollars saved—and if you do sue, I'll deny I ever confided in you. It's not in any bank.'

'Keep your three grand. And you shouldn't carry that kind of money on you,' he felt compelled to add.

'Who says I do? Okay, I'm grabbing my phone from my backpack so I can see what time it is.'

'You have a phone?'

'Yup. Phone, car, computer, and a good pair of secateurs. All my worldly possessions. See why you shouldn't sue me for taking cuttings of your rare plants without permission? Okay, it's eight fifty-two in the evening. Are you hungry? Could you eat a cow?'

'Do you have one of my cows in your backpack too?'

'Dude, I'm hurt by your extreme lack of faith

in my essential goodness, but the answer is no. Not this trip.'

'You're not going to put pictures of me busted up all over the Internet, are you?'

'You think I could sell those for a mint and pay my uni fees?'

He absolutely did think that.

'Oh.' She paused, as if only just realising his accident would be of public interest. 'No, I'm not going to take pictures of you all busted up and sell them to the highest bidder,' she offered quietly. 'I wouldn't do that. If that's what people do in your world, I feel sorry for you.'

He felt the need to explain. 'You wouldn't believe what papers print about me.'

'So you're not crazy in love with your brother's beautiful wife?'

How had that rumour started again? 'Me and m'brother were trying to buy a national energy company a couple of years back. That rumour was a way to disrupt our takeover bid.'

She took her own sweet time thinking about that. 'Your world is brutal,' she declared finally.

'Yes.'

There was another pause, a bigger one, before the voice spoke again. 'She's very beautiful, though. Your sister-in-law.'

'She's also smart, kind and I've known her since birth. Still doesn't mean I'm in love with her.'

'I do have a macadamia and coconut bar I could share with you,' she murmured.

'Keep it.' He was angry with her for believing the lies they wrote about him.

'Hey, you were prepared to believe the worst of me too, Mr Take a picture of me all battered and torn and sell it to the papers and make a mint.'

He had no comeback for that. She was right. But maybe they could start again, right here and now. He reached towards her and his fingers collided with the gently rounded flesh of what was most likely her rear end. He cleared his throat and withdrew his hand. She was a warm presence at his side from shoulder to toe. It was enough. 'Can we start over? I'm not…usually so…tetchy.'

'It's not just you. I'm on edge too and I'm sorry for repeating what the gossip rags were saying. They make stuff up as they go along.'

'True.'

'Would you like some more water?'

'Please.'

She rose from her spot beside him and then he felt the cut of a plastic drink bottle against his lips. He reached up to close his fingers around the bottle and caught her fingers too.

'I've got it,' he murmured.

'Hang on, let me—there. It's all yours.'

He slaked his thirst, and he was uncommonly thirsty.

'Hey, easy with that.' He felt her palm against his forehead, low over his unseeing eyes. 'You're hot.'

'I get that a lot.'

'I bet you do.'

Were they flirting? Was he reading the room right?

She cleared her throat. 'I meant you have a temperature, which isn't exactly wonderful news. I don't think we should wait this one out until someone finds us. I need to go for help.'

'The ridge,' he murmured. 'You'll get a phone signal from up there.'

'Maybe.' The dust might make it impossible. 'But the track's a mess. I passed it on the way here. Thought about going up and decided not to. But I will get up it if need be,' she amended hastily. 'I've done it before.'

'*Have* you now?' No way was she a stranger to this land. 'Take me with you.'

'Hell no. You think I'm going to jolt that head of yours around any more than I have to? What if your eyes are hanging by a thread and the drive up the ridge breaks that thread? You'll never see again.'

He hated that she might be right. 'When will you go?'

'Not tonight. You aren't the only one who can't see two metres in front of them at the moment.'

She sighed heavily. 'I'll leave at dawn. The dust should have settled a bit by then.'

'Don't leave without telling me.'

'I won't.'

She settled into what might have been a companionable silence if Reid hadn't been so hell-bent on filling up his lack of sight with other sensory input. He didn't want to be alone with his thoughts and the pain in his body that threatened to make him weep. 'Talk to me.'

'About what?'

'What's your favourite memory?'

'Why should I give it to you?'

'Because talking about it makes you happy?' He couldn't get to know her without her co-operation and it occurred to him that he really did want to get to know her. She was brave and resourceful. She didn't seem to have an agenda beyond keeping him alive and going for help as soon as possible. She was funny and sensible and unusual and…wonderful to listen to, and maybe it was just because they were under duress that he thought that way and maybe it wasn't. 'C'mon, work with me here. Tell me about the best day you've ever had.'

'Wouldn't you rather I read the textbook to you? We're up to plants beginning with the letter T.'

'Spare me.'

'You first, then.' She moved around and did whatever it was she was doing—taking the blanket she'd had around him away so he could get rid of some body heat, he surmised. But her body stayed in contact with his and he was grateful he didn't have to ask for her touch again. She'd twigged that being without her touch made him panic. 'What's your favourite memory?'

'Watching my brother walk out those prison gates and smile when he saw me.'

'He didn't know you'd be there to collect him?'

'I told him I'd be there. I just don't think he believed it. We got half an hour down the road before I pulled into a service station that had a diner attached to it. I wanted breakfast and asked him what he was having and he just stared at the menu as if he was lost. My big badass brother needed my help with something and I was over the moon about it. I wanted him to like me so bad. He was my hero.'

'Your brother who killed a man was your hero?'

'Exceptional circumstances.' Reid heard his own voice hardening in warning not to press this line of questioning. 'He had to.' No point sharing that Reid was in two minds about whether his brother had pulled that trigger at all. Reid thought Bridie's father might have been the one with the gun in his hand and that Reid had taken the fall so that then sixteen-year-old Bridie wouldn't be left alone in the world. Not that Judah had ever confirmed this. 'He's still my hero—even after all these years.'

'Loyal.' She patted his shoulder as if to reassure him. 'I like that.'

'Why do you keep patting that shoulder?' Why not his chest or his arm or take his hand as she had before.

'It's the only piece of you that isn't bloody, bruised or banged up.'

'That bad?'

'Not good. Keep going with your best day ever. What food did you order in the diner?'

'So, I ended up ordering for both of us, yeah? I was eighteen, fresh out of boarding school and my father had just died and my mother had passed not long before that. I'd been alone on Jeddah station, running it, trying to make sure my brother had somewhere to come home to, and the only people I'd been around for months were Tom Starr from the cattle station next door, and his daughter Bridie, and Gert—the housekeeper who came in three days every fortnight.'

'I heard that story, yeah. You did a good job.'

'I didn't want to fail my brother. I badly wanted to prove to everyone I could do it.'

'I know that feeling.'

He could hear the truth in her quiet words,

even if he couldn't see it in her eyes. His remaining senses seemed so much more acute. 'I couldn't have done it without them. I'm eternally in their debt.' He reached out towards her and she wove her fingers through his and held his hand.

'Touchy-feely guy.'

'Don't tell anyone. I have a reputation to maintain as an emotional desert.'

'Your secret is safe with me.'

Her hands weren't soft. Her nails felt a little ragged and she had calluses at the base of her thumb and fingers. He had the sudden urge to bring her hand to his lips and test the ridges of her knuckles with his tongue. Would she wrest her hand from his?

Or would she acknowledge a deep feeling of familiarity similar to his?

He contented himself with rubbing the pad of his thumb up and down her thumb instead. 'Where were we?'

'Ordering breakfast at the diner. On your best day ever.'

Right. 'I ordered two big breakfast combos, coffee with milk on the side, a banana smoothie each, apple pie, hot chips, tomato sauce, salt and vinegar, and a brownie each. Oh, and a couple of bottles of that blue-coloured sports drink. I had the station credit card in my back pocket and I likely would have kept right on ordering if the woman behind the counter hadn't said, "Son, I think that's enough."'

'Dead straight.'

He smiled, never mind his aching face. 'I dug in like a heathen when the food came and it took me a minute to realise Judah wasn't eating. I thought he wasn't hungry. I figured myself for a fool and started to apologise until he said stop. I told him I just wanted to make a good impression and I was sorry and again he said stop, so I stopped. I thought he was going to get up and walk out.'

'And this is your *best* day ever?'

'It gets better,' he defended. 'Judah had the biggest case of PTSD I've ever seen but he looked at me and somehow he decided to trust me. He said, "Reid, I'm hungry but this is a lot and I haven't made a decision for myself in seven and a half years. I'm gonna need your help."

'"Start with the smoothie and the banana bread," I said, and he laughed, but he did it, and I knew at that moment that he wanted me to stick around and that everything was going to be fine. Sometimes families fracture. I was scared that was going to happen to mine, and then what?'

'I get it. Trust me, I know that playbook by heart.'

Her voice held a wealth of sadness, bedrocked by maturity. He wondered how old she was and whether he'd already asked her that. Was he way off in thinking her a few years younger than him because she was still a student studying for exams? Didn't exactly matter. She understood, and that was enough to crack him wide open.

'The thing about the Blake family set-up is that the firstborn takes all,' he told her gruffly. 'The British barony, all the land. Nothing on Jeddah Creek station or back in the UK was mine. And some time between the banana bread and the bacon and eggs I asked him outright if he wanted me to stick around. Almost lost my breakfast after I'd said it, although that may have had something to do with the way I'd bolted my food.'

'Maybe.' She had the driest laugh. He could listen to it for ever. And she was a good listener too, even if he had almost run out of steam for storytelling. His brain hurt. Everything hurt. 'So did he ask you to stay?'

'Mm-huh. Said there was no way he was walking through this world without me at his side. Best day ever.'

'I like it. Means he'll be coming for you sooner rather than later.'

He liked the way she thought. 'Now you,' he murmured. 'Share.'

'Ack, I don't have any memories like that. My world is small.'

'Tell me anyway.'

'Seeing the coastline for the first time was pretty spectacular. Water all the way to the end of the earth.'

'How old were you?'

'I dunno. About six? Seeing a man-made waterfall and swimming pool in someone's backyard also blew my mind. I would have been in my early teens then. Watching the rain come down out here, looking at the patterns the water makes as it finds its way along.'

He was sensing a water theme. 'Have you ever seen the Bay of Islands in Vietnam? Or the Weeping Wall on Mount Waialeale in Hawaii?'

'Never.'

'I'll take you when we get out of here.'

'Sure you will.' She sounded indulgent.

'I mean it.'

Maybe he did in the here and now, but Ari wasn't stupid enough to think he'd keep his word. They'd patch him up good as new and he wouldn't remember a thing about her.

'Give me another memory. Who's your favourite person?' he asked.

His words were starting to slur, and she desperately wanted him to stay awake, because every time he slipped from consciousness she thought he might never wake again. 'My mother. She passed.'

'Not your father?'

'He's not in my life. My mother never had much to say about anything, least of all him. He was a passing stockman from up north. A charming one-night stand. That's all I know.'

Ari squeezed his hand. He really did respond beautifully to touch. Maybe she'd respond that way too if she couldn't see anything. 'So talking wasn't her thing but she had the most expressive eyes I've ever seen. She could tell me she loved me and was proud of me with a glance. If I ever got a good mark at school, her eyes would show her pride. If I ever made something for her—kid stuff like a wind chime made out of a bunch of sticks held together with baling twine—she'd look at me with such love. When I was thoughtful and careful with what we had, her eyes would smile and she'd nod and I'd know I was loved. Even when—' Not so good, those later memories. 'Even when she married and got really busy and had my little stepbrother and stepfather to look after, she still loved me with her eyes.'

When she could. Ari's stepfather had been a jealous man, always resentful of any love shown to Ari. As if there weren't enough of it to go around...

'I bet she looked at you like that a lot. You have a kind heart.'

'You think so?' Ari made light of his compliment, not wanting to reveal the truth of those later years when her mother would barely look at her at all for fear one of them would end up with a beating. 'Because I've just realised that I've been banging on about visual memories to a guy who currently can't see.'

'I can see blurry shapes,' he offered quietly. 'There's light and dark.'

She didn't have the heart to tell him she'd turned the light off long ago and they were talking in complete darkness. 'I washed some of the blood out of your good eye while you were out for the count.'

'I wish I could see you.'

She didn't know why those few words touched her so deeply. 'Yeah, well. Nothing fancy to see here, but I hope you see again soon. Mind you, if I'm being totally honest, there's something freeing about communicating with you in the dark using words and touch. I feel comfortable here with you like this. Almost as if I'm your equal. I'm not as self-conscious about my looks or the cheap clothes I've got on.'

'I don't judge people by their looks,' he growled.

'Yeah, you do. You were quite happy to picture me as a beautiful Bond girl.'

He swore softly, likely because she had him cornered. 'Well, I don't judge people by their bank balance,' he said next.

'Sure, you do. We all do, and the world is poorer for it.' She lay back beside him, shoulder to shoulder in the cramped little tent, and listened for his breathing. 'What's your favourite musical instrument? Mine's guitar. I can't read music or anything and I'm pretty sure I don't have perfect pitch. Nor can I listen to a song and play it from memory, but I like having a bash anyway.'

'Describe your mother's eyes whenever you played guitar.' His voice was getting weaker.

'Who knows? She always got as far away as she could so she didn't have to listen to it.'

'Funny girl.'

She closed her eyes and tried to figure out the blends that went into the making of his voice. Warmth wrapped around a core of pain that likely wasn't always present. Occasional sharpness that came with anger. A burr full of humour, pricking at a person's ears at unexpected times. Curiosity—how could a person explain the sound of curiosity? But it was there. She liked his voice a lot. Always had, even when she was a kid.

Not that she'd ever crushed on him as a kid— he'd been so much older, but still. The teenage boy with the ready smile hadn't lost his kindness.

'Who are you?' he rasped, and she was about to tell him she was Ari, Ari Cohen, his housekeeper's niece, and she'd tagged along with her aunt sometimes as a kid and met him way back when.

But he was already unconscious again.

Ari rose with the dawn and gently shook Reid semi-awake. He didn't seem to know where he was at all but she'd promised not to leave without saying goodbye and she also took the opportunity to feed him two more painkillers and get him to drink some water. She left the mostly full water bottle near his uninjured hand, although even that had swollen overnight.

'Reid, I'm heading up to the escarpment now. I'll be back as soon as I can.'

She rubbed his shoulder but he didn't rouse. One eye had swollen shut altogether and his other remained closed. His temperature had stayed up and she'd taken to pouring water on his bandages to cool him down, but it wasn't enough to stop his fever. He needed proper medical care.

She pressed her lips to his cheek for no other reason than if he died from his injuries, she wanted his last human touch to honour love.

In dawn's half-light she packed her ute and turned the key, and, after a few coughs and splutters, the engine roared to life. She'd been worried it wouldn't start because of the dust she'd driven through to reach Reid, but it seemed okay. *Sweetie, don't fail me now.* She set out towards the escarpment, following no track whatsoever, because she'd gone off road to find him and off road she would stay until she picked up the trail.

Five minutes later, she stopped to let some air out of her tyres before setting off again at a much slower pace.

Yesterday's dust storm had deposited a fine, silty covering over everything, and it was deeper than expected. Three hours, she estimated, before she got where she needed to go, and another three hours back to the tent.

Had to be done.

Reid's life depended on it.

She was two hours into her journey and she'd reached the foot of the escarpment and found the track that would take her to the top when she saw the helicopter in the distant sky. She skidded her ute to a halt, her heart thumping with hope that they would see the crash site uphill and the tent, or if they missed it that they would see her, and she could try and wave them down and give them directions.

But they didn't come her way, they circled back and forth in grid-like fashion, causing Ari to scream with frustration and begin mouthing directions they couldn't hear. She got out of the car and began waving her arms, before reaching back in the cab for a bright red pullover so she could wave that too.

Head south, now southwest. That's it, you've got this. West. I meant west! Now, straighten up and just keep going.

If she willed it maybe it would happen.

That's it. Yes. Yes!

They'd seen it. They'd found him.

Ari flung her fists towards the sky. 'Yes!' Hurry. 'He's waiting for you.'

The stress of the past twenty-four hours hit her like a truck, and she sank to the ground and put her hands to her face and sobbed her relief, letting go of the fear that whatever she did, it wouldn't be enough. He'd get the best of care now, and it *would* be enough.

Hours later, when Ari made it back to camp, there was nothing left but her tent on its side, her sleeping bag still wet with blood and a helicopter in pieces.

They'd come for him and taken him.

Wounded billionaire and test helicopter pilot Reid Blake was gone.

CHAPTER FOUR

'I THINK YOU should come. You need the work and the Blakes can always use a spare set of hands.' Gert stood at her kitchen counter, packing cleaning supplies into neatly labelled plastic tubs. She looked up and arched a winged brow, as if daring Ari to refuse.

'You told me the caterers always bring their own staff with them.' The Jeddah Creek station ball, hosted by Bridie and Judah Blake, had become an annual event these past dozen years or so, getting grander every year. 'And they fly bar staff in as well.'

'True.'

'Then what is there for me to do?'

'None of them get to go back of house. You'll be helping me with the guest rooms and bathrooms and making the special guests staying at the homestead comfortable. You know the layout of the house and, more to the point, Judah and Bridie know you. They can trust you.'

Could they? Ari had never come forward to say she'd found Reid and looked after him until proper help arrived—that was six months ago now. Practically ancient history.

She'd been meaning to contact them as soon as she got back to town, but as one day had slid into the next and there'd been no word of Reid at all, she hadn't wanted to 'fess up and potentially be blamed for not doing more and sooner.

Or try to explain to big brother Judah exactly what she'd been doing out there in the first place.

It wasn't as if Reid would ever be able to identify her, even if he did have vague memories of her being there. Maybe she *could* go with Gert and see this dazzling Outback spectacle of beautiful people in an opulent setting for herself? 'So who are the special guests?'

Gert shrugged. 'Don't know for sure. It's all very hush-hush until they get there. We had a European prince and princess last year. Very polite.'

Ari blinked. 'Seriously?'

'Yep. And a grand dame of the English theatre—I can't remember her name, but you'd know her if you saw her. Barking, of course, but she told the funniest stories.'

'How many guest bedrooms do they put out for use?'

'Six. And two drawing rooms for only those house guests to retreat to, plus the library. So twelve guests in the house, maximum, and around five hundred outside in tents, vehicles and planes.'

'Five...*hundred*?'

'But you don't have to worry about them. Judah's station hands run herd on them.'

Still no mention of Reid or whether he would be present. Last she'd heard, he'd been released from hospital and was living in Sydney.

'You can sleep in my room with me, there's two single beds,' Gert continued. She'd had the use of that room for near on thirty years and had no qualms about treating it as her own. 'And you can give me a hand with the Sunday breakfast barbecue. Reid and his old boarding-school mates usually tackle that one, but not this year.'

'Oh, is he not coming?' See an opening and take it, guileless as you please.

'He'll be there, he just won't be helping out the way he usually does. But it's easy enough to do. Steak, sausages, bacon, eggs, onion, bread rolls, lettuce, tomato and a few different types of sauce. Hangover food. Breakfast is very popular.'

'I'll bet.' Ari risked another question. 'And how is Reid after his accident?' The Blake family had kept news of his recovery so hush-hush. It drove her nuts.

'Better than he was. It was touch and go for a while.'

'I didn't know that.'

Gert tucked half a dozen packs of cleaning wipes into the nearest container, alongside four litres of bathroom disinfectant concentrate. 'So, do you want the work or not? I'm getting old waiting for your answer.'

Gert was already old. She'd been doing the Devil's Kiss, Jeddah Creek, and Cooper's Crossing station houses cleaning run for thirty years. She spent two to three days on each farm, with a day's driving in between each. She would then return home for a long weekend break before loading up the van and looping around again. Gert and her van full of refrigerated foodstuffs and cleaning equipment and mail were as much a part of the Outback landscape as the cattle stations themselves.

'I'll even stop so you can collect plants along the way,' Gert coaxed.

'I'll believe that when it happens.' Gert drove as if the devil were riding her tail and rarely stopped for anything or anyone.

'Still waiting.' Gert smiled and the sternness bled out of her, leaving warmth in its wake. 'Don't make me start tapping my foot.'

'All right, all right, I'll come.' Ari could observe Reid Blake from afar as he mingled with the stars. And even if they did cross paths, he probably wouldn't speak. And what was the chance of him recognising her voice from their time in the tent, given he'd spent most of that time drifting in and out of consciousness? No, she had nothing to worry about on that score.

She could see for herself how he was getting on, lay new memories over more disturbing ones and then put him out of her mind altogether.

Maybe then she wouldn't be so obsessed with remembering every little thing about him. Fantasising. Measuring every other man she met against him and finding them wanting.

Not touchy-feely enough. Not interesting enough.

Not vulnerable enough to seek out an honest connection, her brutally honest conscience suggested.

Face it, Ari. You liked being in a position of power over Reid Blake. It made you bolder and him more receptive.

Which he wouldn't be now he was well again. He'd probably want nothing to do with her even if he did recognise her. The man in the tent probably didn't even *exist.*

Probably a good thing. That way she might stop *pining* for him.

'What's the pay rate?'

'As my trusty assistant? How about we ask for twenty-five dollars an hour from the time you get there until the time you leave, including when you're asleep?'

'Are you serious? That's a six-hundred-dollar day.' Before tax. And with her ute at the mechanic's and needing a new radiator, she could use all the cash she could get. 'How many days will we be there?'

That there was Gert's gotcha smile. 'Three.'

CHAPTER FIVE

'You do it,' said Judah, as if his word were law. And, okay, maybe Judah was the oldest and this was his home and Reid was a mere guest here these days, but *come on*.

Reid had turned thirty last year. He'd been a billionaire in his own right since his mid-twenties, on account of his relentless quest to make solar-powered commercial plane travel possible. And he had absolutely no trouble whatsoever questioning his big brother's authority. Even if they had just entered the library, where several centuries of Blake family history lay gathering dust at every opportunity. He crossed to the unlit fireplace to lean against the mantelpiece, unwilling to show how much his leg ached this early in the evening.

Judah would only worry more than he already did.

Reid accepted the tumbler of twenty-year-old malt whisky Judah handed him and raised it to his lips for a hit of fortification before returning to the argument. 'You're the one with the title,' he said with possibly a little too much relish, because with that title came onerous responsibilities. 'You're head of the family. It needs to come from you.'

It was the afternoon of the twelfth annual Jeddah Creek station ball and already people were rolling in and setting up camp in the paddocks beyond the homestead. Caterers had taken over the mess hall and kitchen that the station hands usually used, and one end of the grand ballroom was in the process of being turned into a fully stocked drinks bar that would be the envy of any big city hotel. Every little detail concerning the glamorous society event had been hammered out months ago. Every last detail but for who would make the welcome speech and expose a family secret that had been hidden for years.

'If I make the announcement, no one's ever going to come forward,' argued Judah. 'They'll probably think I'll murder them.'

'Bull. You haven't murdered anyone in years.' If indeed his brother ever had been responsible for the loss of a man's life. 'Besides, it was self-defence.'

'The fact remains that you're far more approachable than I am.' Judah was having none of it. '*And* people want to see you in action after the accident. They want to know you're up and running, full speed ahead.'

'I'm here, aren't I?' Reid was beginning to lose this argument, he could tell. 'All you have to say is that it's recently come to our attention that we have a half-sister out there and we want to find her. Simple.'

The thud of something falling to the floor reached his ears and both he and Judah turned towards the direction of the noise. Was someone else in the room? He couldn't see anyone—not that his eyesight was all that reliable when the lights were dim. Or when the lights were bright, for that matter. But this part of the house was supposedly off-limits to the catering team, bar staff and musicians who'd flown in this morning, and as far as he knew Judah's house guests had yet to arrive.

'Who's there?' asked Judah sharply.

'Awkward,' came the muffled reply, and then a hand rose from behind the couch, followed by the outline of a young woman who looked to be barely out of her teens. When she stood up, she had a little dustpan and broom in her other hand, half full of broken glass. 'Hi,' she said weakly. 'Gert sent me to clear up a broken vase and so here I am. I was doing that when you came in so I just...' she waved her free hand about '...decided not to interrupt your very important conversation.'

'Gert sent you?' Something didn't add up. 'And who are you?' She seemed familiar. More than that, she sounded familiar. That bright, melodic voice was like a burr beneath his skin.

'I'm Ari. Ari Cohen.'

Was that supposed to ring a bell?

'Gert's niece,' she said next, looking from him to Judah. 'She said you wouldn't mind an extra set of hands back here today, so here I am. Bridie okayed it. I used to come here with Gert when I was a kid. She used to take us kids on her cleaning run sometimes in the school holidays and stuff.'

'And stuff,' he echoed quietly. It was true that Gert had often brought various nieces and nephews along for the ride, but that was a long time ago.

Memory pinged of a barefoot little girl who'd attacked dusty windows with a dirty dry rag and uncommon zeal. Once finished for the day she'd entertained herself by making racetracks in the dirt if she'd brought her matchbox cars with her. And if she'd forgotten those little cars, or lost them, she'd turn her hand to making pictures in the dirt using whatever came to hand. More than once, she'd ventured way too far from the homestead looking for different coloured dirt and Gert had sent Reid out to find her. He'd been in his teens and she'd been, what, seven or eight? 'You used to make the rock gardens.'

'That's me.' She smiled, and more memories came rushing in.

That smile.

That wide, cheerful smile she used to offer so freely for no good reason other than the sun was shining and she had company. He turned to his brother. 'Do you remember her? They might have been your prison years.'

Young Ari snorted and drew his gaze away from Judah.

'You didn't remember me either until I reminded you, hotshot, so don't go getting too carried away with how smart you are.'

Judah's cough sounded suspiciously like laughter.

Reid ignored his brother's rare lapse of composure. 'How much did you overhear?'

'All of it,' said Ari. 'I'm not deaf.'

Which for some strange reason set Judah off again.

Again, Reid ignored him in favour of the admittedly pretty young woman with the dustpan in hand. 'Who do *you* think should give the speech?'

'Hey, I'm just the hired help. Don't ask me.'

Her voice… He rubbed at the scar tissue at

his hairline. It still gave him trouble, still itched abominably at the oddest times.

'Although your brother's probably right about people wanting to see for themselves that you're okay. You're kind of important around here,' she continued. 'Why can't you both stand up and have one of you welcome everyone and then the other one gets down to business? Everyone likes a united family front.'

Reid caught Judah's eye and spread his hands out, palm up. 'Makes sense.'

Something thumped against a solid surface and Reid sensed movement in his peripheral vision. 'What was that?'

Ari swung around towards a window with velvet curtains bunched and tied on either side. '*That* is the reason I'm in here in the first place. I have orders to lock him in the upstairs ensuite bathroom when I catch him. He escaped. We think human error was involved.'

Judah cleared his throat loudly.

Reid had no idea what was going on. 'Him? As in a person? As opposed to a…?'

'Kitten,' she said cheerfully. 'A fluffy, grey, tawny-eyed agent of chaos. He likes escaping from locked bathrooms, knocking over vases and hiding behind curtains.'

Reid turned to his brother. 'You have a house cat?'

'It wasn't my idea.'

Reid knew exactly whose idea it would have been. 'Does my niece have a kitten? Did the lord of the realm let the itty-bitty kitty out of the bathroom?'

Judah winced and scraped his weathered hand over his face. 'I don't want to talk about it.'

'Does the kitty have a name?'

'Fluffy.'

'I'm sorry, I didn't hear you on account of your hand being over your mouth.' Life was good today, what with Ari the desert nymph gracing them with her delightful presence and seeming so familiar, and now Judah wincing with embarrassment. 'What was that again?'

'Fluffy.' Judah silently dared him to laugh, but Reid would never. Not even a smirk. Okay, maybe Reid was wearing a *tiny* smirk to go with his white shirt, and immaculately cut suit. 'Does Fluffy have a last name? Fluffy Blake? Fluffy Woo?'

'No.' Judah looked truly pained by the turn this conversation had taken, which pleased Reid no end. 'Fluffy-Wuffy.'

Fluffy-Wuffy was currently being stalked by the lithe, long-legged, black-trousers-and-T-shirt-clad Ari with the high ponytail. She moved with the grace of a dancer—maybe she *was* one when she wasn't cleaning houses, she was slender enough. Long neck. Delicate hands that parted the curtain and reached down and scooped up a little blob that meowed in protest.

'Oh, stop your complaining,' she murmured, and something about her *voice* was so familiar…

She was a local.

The woman who'd found him in a dust storm and erected a tent over the top of him had been local.

'What kind of car do you drive?' he asked as she tucked the kitten against her chest and headed for the door.

'I'm currently carless. I got a lift here with Gert. So…excuse me, it was nice to catch up, but I have to put the monster away.'

'Will I see you around, later?' He didn't want her to go. A familiar word sat on the tip of his tongue.

Stay. Don't leave me.

'I don't know,' she replied as she half turned and met his gaze and this time he was close enough to make out the colour of her eyes. They were an extraordinary shade of cognac and quite startling against her tanned complexion. 'I hope you find your sister.'

She took her leave, and he waited until he no longer heard her footsteps on the stairs before he spoke again. 'What colour would you say her hair was?'

'Brown.' Judah had grown used to Reid asking him to describe in detail those things Reid couldn't see properly.

'And her eyes? What colour are they?'

'Brown,' said Judah again. 'Why?'

'Just curious.'

Very, very curious.

Speech plans sorted, Reid downed his drink, abandoned his brother and made his way to the kitchen in search of Gert. The housekeeper had been a mainstay throughout his childhood and he was as sure of his welcome as anyone could be, even if she did greet him with a steely eye to match her greying hair and a curt, 'You're too thin.'

'I'm working on it, I promise,' and it was nothing but the truth. 'I do physio three days a week to strengthen my leg and drink the most disgusting protein shakes for breakfast every morning, along with my three-course breakfast.'

'Three cups of black coffee is not a three-course breakfast,' Gert countered. She knew him too well.

'Even so, I've picked up my calorie intake, on doctor's orders, and I'm feeling stronger for it.' He'd been incredibly lucky to survive at all.

'How's your eyesight?'

'Good as gold.' No one wanted to hear about the fuzzy vision in one eye and the tunnel vision in the other. The constant headaches. His dodgy balance. His chances of ever piloting a helicopter again were slim, even by his optimistic reckoning. Without bionic eyes.

As he was a man of unlimited resources, bionic eye research was now a priority for Reid Enterprises' newly created Medical Division.

'I met up with Ari in the library just now. I didn't recognise her, though, until she told me who she was.'

Let Gert make of that what she would. Could be his eyesight. Could be that he hadn't seen her in years.

'Did she find that cat?'

'You mean Fluffy-Wuffy?' He was never going to pass up the chance to say that name aloud, just to see his brother wince. 'She found him. *Fluffy-Wuffy* is on his way back to jail.'

'She's a good girl, Ari. The first in our family to study for a diploma, and it's not because learning comes easily to her—it's because she never gives up.'

'An admirable trait.' The acquisition of Ari information was going to be easier than he thought. 'What's she studying?'

'Some kind of land-care course. Landscape gardening. Horticulture too, which will be good for her. She's not one for staying indoors.'

It fitted. Everything about her fitted his mystery rescuer from the tent. 'I remember that about her.'

'She sits her last two exams in a couple of weeks and then there's a job waiting for her in Cairns.'

'Doing what?'

'She'll be a nursery worker in a big native plant nursery and landscaping business.'

'Does it have a career pathway for her?'

'Ask her,' said Gert as Ari swept into the room and stopped abruptly at the sight of him.

'Ask me what?'

'How wedded you are to your new job,' he said smoothly. 'Gert's been bragging about your studies.' Did Ari look a little paler than before? He couldn't trust his eyes. 'And it reminded me I've been meaning to advertise for a landscaper to extend the outdoor areas around the eco lodges. There's fifteen of them scattered throughout Jeddah Creek and Cooper's Crossing, mainly in groups of twos and threes.' His information was solid. Factual. But he was making up the job on the spot.

'I'm not set up to be an independent contractor just yet,' she said awkwardly as she reached for a tea towel and picked up a handful of wet silverware from the counter. Family crest and all.

'Is being your own boss a long-term goal?' he asked next.

She nodded warily.

'She wants to have a big Outback plant nursery one day and breed rare native plants. Tell him, Ari,' Gert urged. 'You talked about it enough on the way here.'

'Yeah, Ari. Spill.'

If anything, she grew even paler. 'It was just talk.'

It was her. It had to be her. His eyes couldn't confirm it, but his body seemed to yearn for the comfort of her touch. She was his mystery woman, his guardian angel. He'd been looking for her for months. Visiting her over and over again in his dreams and now here she was, pretending none of it had ever happened. Her reticence made him want to push and tear and, above all, touch. Why had she never come forward? He needed to know. He needed to fix this.

'So, you're a rare plant collector? How does that work?'

Her eyes flashed with a mixture of fear and defiance. She knew he was onto her.

Did she really think he was going to do anything but thank her? Reward her for her bravery? He wouldn't *be* here if she hadn't found him and kept him safe until the medics arrived.

'Blake Holdings—that's a company me and my brother formed—it provides research grants and accommodation for people who want to study habitat and wildlife out here. Landscape ecology and the like. That includes plants.'

'Yeah, for people with fancy degrees and doctorates,' she said, not meeting his gaze. 'I don't even have a tech diploma.'

'Yet,' he said quietly, and her pretty mouth firmed, and she nodded, even if she still wouldn't look at him.

'Yet,' she echoed.

He knew that voice. It kept him company in his dreams. 'You got the Cairns job, didn't you? Put down what you told them.'

'It's a *junior nursery hand* position.'

'Don't you want to jump in the deep end?' She hesitated and with that he moved closer to where he could see better. 'I couldn't see your eyes properly from over there.' They stood about a metre apart. Close enough for him to see her ridiculously long eyelashes and every emotion flitting across her expressive eyes. 'Is this too close? Tell me if it is.' It wasn't for him. They'd been closer in the tent, and not just in a physical sense. He wanted that again.

'No.' But she folded her arms across her chest, and he didn't need to be a body language expert to know that she was putting up barriers against him. He wanted to touch her so badly—one touch and he'd know for sure…

Instead, he kept his hands to himself, took a

careful step back, and returned to his sales pitch. 'The way I see it, going into business for yourself requires three things.

'One: a bone-deep belief that you can do it.'

She lifted her chin and finally met his gaze. Had she really described herself as plain? Because between those eyes, that generous mouth, and her perfectly proportioned form she was anything but.

Was he really shallow enough to be pleased that the woman from the tent was brave, resourceful, *within his grasp* and beautiful in a way that was wholly unique and exactly to his taste?

Yes—yes, he was.

'Two,' he continued firmly, and shoved his shallowness aside, 'you need courage in the face of adversity and the ability to improvise. Anything happen to you lately to demonstrate that? Anything you want to mention? Anything at all?' That's right, Ari Cohen, I know what you're made of. I was there when you were tested.

'Is this a job interview?'

'And three,' he continued his pitch. 'It helps to have deep pockets.'

'Tapping out.' She huffed a laugh. 'Thanks for the tips. I'll keep them in mind.'

'If you don't have start-up money there are angel investors who—if you present a strong enough case—will invest in you and your business dreams.' Surely she could see what he was offering? 'You could ask me to back you.'

'No.' Her hands stilled on the cutlery. 'I'm not ready for that kind of responsibility. I don't know enough yet. I need to work with good growers and plant breeders and that's what I'm going to do. Then maybe I'll get to that bone-deep certainty you mentioned. I don't have it yet.'

'You know where to find me when you do. And if there's anything you want to talk with me about this weekend, I'm free.'

'I'm on the clock.'

He wanted to break the clock.

Was she the woman from the tent? She fitted every memory he had of the event.

He'd made no secret of the fact that someone had tended to him and then gone for help before the helicopters arrived. He'd put out a nationwide call for them to come forward and be rewarded.

Why hadn't she come forward?

'That's very generous of you, Reid.' It wasn't Ari who spoke. It was Gert.

Ari nodded but said nothing.

He made his way to the door, grateful he no longer had to use a cane for walking and that he could see far enough these days to avoid walking into walls. A man had his pride, even in the face of rejection. Especially in the face of rejection.

Why hadn't she come when he called?

'What was that?'

Gert was no one's fool, no matter how wide and innocent Ari made her eyes. 'Kind of intense, isn't he?' she replied. 'Is he always so… helpful?'

'Reid always helps if he can, that's just his way. *Noblesse oblige.* He was born to it.' Gert filled an electric hot-water urn sitting on the counter with bottled water from a thirty-litre container. 'This has to go to the green drawing room on the ground floor.'

'Got it. Have you seen the paddocks?' Anything to avoid talking about her unsettling encounter with Reid. Or admitting to herself how much she'd wanted to reach out and take his hand and say something utterly ridiculous like *hi, it's me.* 'All those planes nose to tail in neat little rows. And there's a campground full of fancy tents with sisal carpets and solar fairy lights mixing it with farm four-wheel drives and campfires and swags. And the portable toilet blocks and the first-aid tent. It's like a festival.'

'It's grown over the years, just like everything the Blake brothers touch.' Gert studied her with a frown. 'Reid just offered you the kind of opportunity you've always dreamed of doing and you turned him down flat.'

'Didn't feel right.' Ari wrapped the cord around the urn and positioned the unwieldy cylinder for pickup. She'd barely wrapped her arms around the body, taps to the outside, when her aunt spoke again.

'They say he died on the way to the hospital.'

'What?' She had no air left in her lungs and the urn was far heavier than it looked. She'd convinced herself in the days that followed the accident that no one who talked and flirted and had shown up for her the way Reid had in the tent could be that badly injured. That thought had soothed her to sleep some nights. And she'd been *wrong*?

'Bridie told me. It's not general knowledge but his heart stopped three times while they were in the air. They got him back, obviously.'

Obviously.

'Reid's always been one for a laugh—even when the going got tough. Especially then,' Gert mused. 'He had a lot of responsibility laid on him at a young age, didn't have a choice, and I believe it was the making of him. But he was strong to begin with. I think he sees the same kind of strength in you.'

Ari slid the urn back on the counter. It was

heavy. She wasn't ready for a Gert interrogation. 'He doesn't even know me.'

But that wasn't strictly true given their time together during the storm.

Reid had been having a whole different conversation with her from the one Gert had heard.

'Those eco lodges were his first business win. They still matter to him. You have two weeks until your exams and almost a month before you have to start that nursery job. You could do up garden plans for all those lodges before you go. At least take a look at them and submit something for his consideration. What if you wow him, and all those other fancy people who stay in them learn your name? You couldn't ask for a better start to your career.'

'He didn't mean it.' He'd been digging for a confession or maybe dangling a reward for services rendered. His 'investing' in her had nothing to do with her potential and everything to do with gratitude.

'Yes, he did. He meant every word. You should at least consider it.'

CHAPTER SIX

IT WAS HER. The angel with the tent and the bandages and the painkillers that had saved his life and sanity. His rescuer who'd touched him when he'd needed it and spoken on demand, laying out pieces of her life for him to pick over, even as he'd offered up his most treasured moments for viewing. She'd left him to go get help, he knew that. But then Judah had arrived, and she'd returned to an empty tent.

There'd been no tent, no trace of anyone at all when a field team had returned to clean up the crash site. It was as if she'd never been there at all.

In the six months since the accident no one had ever come forward.

'I found her,' he told his brother when Judah rounded him up for speech time.

'Our missing sister?'

Judah was apparently not a mind-reader. '*No*, the woman from the tent.'

Judah eyed him warily and not without good cause. He'd sat through Reid's delirious ramblings about *the voice*. He'd sat vigil in hospital, baffled when Reid had finally roused and demanded the hand, only to be told *Not that hand... the other hand*!

Later, at Reid's insistence, Judah had given an interview to the local paper expressing the family's gratitude to the unnamed person who'd tended Reid during the dust storm.

'I've found her. The woman who saved my life. It's Gert's niece. Ari.'

'She told you this?'

'No. Well, not exactly, but everything fits. If I could just get her in a dark room and touch her and make her talk to me, I could be absolutely sure.'

'There's a winning plan—if you want to go up on assault charges.' Judah laughed, short and sharp, and then caught his eye. 'Oh, hell. You mean it.'

'It's the only way to know.'

'Or you could just ask her if she was the woman with the tent.' Judah's voice of reason held no sway with Reid.

'I've given her every opportunity to come clean. I've baited her...'

Judah frowned. 'Why?'

'I've offered her work. Grant money. Accommodation. I *created* a position for her. Which she didn't accept.' Was his irritation visible? He thought it might be visible. He'd had so much less patience with the world since his accident. When opportunity came someone's way, the smart thing to do was grab hold with both hands and *take it*. 'Why wouldn't she *take it*?' His vision blurred.

'Reid. *Reid*.'

'What?' His irritation was very definitely visible.

'Chill. You don't even know if it's her.'

'I *do* know it's her.'

'You weren't conscious when we found you. Your temperature was off the charts. One of only two completely terrifying moments of my life. Three, if I count the birth of my daughter, which I should.'

He appreciated the sentiment, but… 'It's her.'

'Then sit down and talk to her. But not right now,' Judah added as Bridie joined them, a vision of woodland loveliness in her sleeveless ballgown that matched the colours of sunset over an Outback sky. 'We have a speech to make. I greet people. You tell people we have a sister out there somewhere and we're looking to find her.'

'Yeah, bring on the imposters.' There would be plenty of those. 'Hey, Bridie.'

His sister-in-law smiled gently. 'Ready to spill?'

It hadn't been an easy decision to reveal their late father's infidelity to the world and openly search for their unknown half-sister. They had one big-money withdrawal as evidence, along with two letters Bridie had unearthed last year when renovating the wine cellar. She could be anyone, anywhere. They'd debated long and hard about searching for her privately, but the truth was they'd run out of leads. 'I'm ready.' He pasted on a smile.

The sooner they got it over with, the sooner he could go find Ari.

With all guest rooms prepared, the library set up with extra refreshments, and the sitting rooms made over into mini retreats for the house guests, Gert let Ari loose to check on the caterer's preparations. Nothing to do with Ari wanting a glimpse of the beautiful ballroom all decked out and filled with beautiful people.

Ari found the event co-ordinator Gert had pointed out to her at the far end of the bar, counting cartons of wine and checking a list. 'Hi, I'm Ari, homestead staff. I've been sent to see if there's anything I can help you with.'

The woman smiled and tucked her pen through the top of the clipboard and then held out her hand. 'Lilah Connor, and thanks for the offer but I have the kitchen in the bunkroom running a treat and the ballroom, downstairs powder rooms and veranda areas covered. Anything beyond that is not my jurisdiction. There are parties out in the car park, *plane* park, and they're getting wilder by the minute. We are *not* the ones serving alcohol out there. Those planes flew in *stocked*.'

'Got it. I'll have a word with the bosses.' Meaning she'd tell Gert, who would relay the information upriver. 'The food looks like it's holding up well. Probably because of all those well-stocked planes.'

Lila shot her a conspiratorial smile. 'Maybe. Other than that, my team has everything under control. It's a fantastic setting for a party. The sunset and the red dirt and the fairy lights and the music and everyone dressed for the cover of *Vogue* magazine. I've never seen anything like it and I've catered a lot of A-list parties in beautiful locations.'

'Something else, isn't it?' A magical wonderland of beautiful indulgence.

A mini orchestra played from a wooden stage at one end of the ballroom. Elegant couples who knew how to waltz made the most of the floorspace available to them. Wall sconces splayed golden light around the edges of the room, throwing flattering light over those gathered around the edges of the dance floor.

'You, girl!' A florid man in a suit two sizes smaller than him waved her over and Lilah went with her. He turned towards the woman at his side. 'My wife isn't feeling well. She needs to lie down.'

'There's a first-aid station set up in the sitting room at the end of the veranda. It's this way,' said Lilah. 'I can escort you and we can get her checked out.'

'She needs a bed, not a Band-Aid,' he snapped. 'She almost fainted when they made the announcement.'

Ari hadn't been in the room during any announcement and looked to Lilah for help.

'You mean about the missing sister?' Lilah asked.

'Yes, yes! Look at her—don't you see the resemblance?'

Reid and Judah were both tall, dark-haired, and lanky. This woman was a tiny, generously rounded blonde.

'She needs a room in the *house*,' the husband insisted. 'We need to speak with *Lord Blake*.'

'I'll…find him,' Ari murmured.

'I'll stay here,' Lilah offered. 'Ma'am, let's find you a seat over by the wall, and a glass of water while we wait.' She and Ari shared a glance—

they were doing their best to be accommodating but this was beyond what either of them had signed up for.

Ari plunged into the crowd and headed towards the front of the ballroom. She searched for Judah and Bridie.

Reid found her first.

'Ari.'

'Hey.' As if beautiful suit-wearing billionaires called her by name all the time. Her body tensed as she met his gaze and something clicked into place, some missing piece of the puzzle that could teach her about passion and obsession. Irresistible fascination with another human being. She had no doubt she could learn such things from him. She just didn't know if she *wanted* to go all in on him. He was Reid Blake and she was nobody.

'There's a guest with a sick wife who almost fainted at your announcement. They're over by the second set of French doors from the bar. He's belligerent and she's scared witless. He's demanding to speak with your brother and he wants a bed in the house for his wife.'

Reid passed a hand over his eyes, his fingers rubbing at a spot on his hairline. She could see the scarring, still puffy, not old enough to have faded to silver. 'I knew this would happen.' He reached inside his jacket and pulled out a phone.

Ari began to drift away, job done, but he reached out and grasped her bare arm. *'Stay.'*

His gaze didn't leave hers as he spoke into the phone. 'We have our first contender.' He gave Judah the directions and ended the call. 'Come with me.' Without waiting for an answer, he slid his hand down her arm, laced his fingers through hers and began weaving through the crowd, with Ari at his side. The warmth and tingle of his hand in hers crashed through her defences, bringing with it memories of their time in the tent. That magical, terrible time when their defences were down and they'd connected with each other in ways she'd never imagined opening up to another person. *'I knew it.'*

'You sound like a crazy person.'

'You know exactly what I'm talking about— you're not that good an actor and unlike last time *I can see you.* I think you must have your mother's eyes. They're *very* expressive.'

He led her through to the long hallway that ran the length of the ground floor. Past the library, past the various bedrooms and sitting rooms until they reached the door at the very end. It was locked but the press of his thumb on a touch- pad opened it to reveal an office decked out in burgundy velvet. Bookshelves, a massive wal- nut desk, an elaborate Aubusson floor rug and dozens of other examples of generational wealth.

'I hope this isn't your idea of cosy and informal.' Seriously, could there be a bigger contrast between this room and her tent? Did he really think she needed reminding of her *place*?

'This was my grandfather's office. Judah needs to redecorate.' He released her hand and Ari shivered at the sudden loss of warmth. He pulled the visitor's chair away from the desk. 'Sit.'

Did she want to defy him in this or save her fire for bigger battles? She sat, and he took the boss chair on the other side of the desk, but not before he'd shut the office door, plunging them into semi-darkness. The only light in the room came from the fairy lights in the trees outside the one narrow window at the opposite end of the room.

'Talk to me,' he commanded.

'I don't know what to say.'

'How about you tell me why you never came forward? Start there.'

There was no give in his voice. None. And she still didn't know what to say.

'You left without saying goodbye,' he continued. 'Not that I want to appear needy, but when it comes to you, I am diabolically needy-feeling. You promised to wake me.'

'I did wake you.' She'd kept her promise. 'You were delirious with fever. I did everything I could for you, you have to know that. I tried to help you. I did help you. What more do you want from me?'

'You left me.'

'To get help. I did not abandon you, I wanted you found. I was so happy when I saw them coming for you.'

His eyes blazed, caught on hers and held. A frisson of awareness snaked through her. She was craving his nearness, wanting his touch again, for reasons other than comfort.

Maybe this was way she'd never come forward.

She hadn't wanted to try and recreate the closeness they'd shared in the tent and not find it again. 'Can we turn on a light?'

He gestured towards the light switch by the door. 'Be my guest.'

The overhead fluorescent lights gave off a bright daytime glow. Ari blinked. Reid reached for a pair of sunglasses tucked into the handkerchief pocket of his jacket. Moments later the dark glasses hid his eyes from view.

'I'm still not good with bright light,' he offered by way of explanation.

'I'm really glad they fixed you. I've been wanting to know the details. I had that in the "reasons to reveal myself" column.'

'You made lists for and against coming forward? I'd like to see that.'

'It's not something I carry on me.' Or that he ever needed to see. 'How's your arm?'

'Pinned in two places, so it's a good thing I never have to rope another steer.'

'And your leg?'

'They used new surgical techniques to help with muscle regeneration.'

'And your head?'

He raked his hand through unruly hair, pushing it back to reveal a spiderweb of jagged scarring still pink against his otherwise tanned skin. 'They pulled a bunch of metal fragments from my head. It hasn't affected brain function so far, although after tonight Judah might beg to differ. The optic nerve in my left eye is permanently damaged but it could have been worse. If I'd stayed in the tent much longer it would have been worse.'

She nodded. 'I left at daybreak. The dust…' No way could she have left any earlier.

'I'm grateful, Ari. Why do you think I've been looking for you all this time? I want to pay you back. I owe you my life, and I am filthy rich and very well connected so if there's anything you want or need, *ask*.'

'I'm not really into payback. Look, I'm glad that you've made such a strong recovery and that I didn't do anything to make things worse. That's a load off my mind.' She still had nightmares about his face. 'If you don't mind me doing a bit of seed collecting in the area, and sometimes I might take cuttings—that'd be awesome. I'm not doing any damage and you said you wouldn't sue.'

'I won't sue.'

'Then that's all I need by way of thank you.'

'I don't believe you. Where's your ute?'

'Getting fixed. The radiator's busted but they found a second-hand one for me. It's under control.'

'Are you digging into your savings to pay for it?'

He remembered that conversation? 'Not after working for your brother this weekend. The hourly rate is generous.' She hated the sunglasses because they hid his eyes, so she stared at his hands instead. They were big and lean, much like the rest of him He kept his nails short and the watch on his wrist looked understated in a way that probably meant it was worth a fortune.

'Let me buy you a new twin cab,' he pressed. 'You'll need something reliable if you're going to be driving back and forth from Cairns.'

'No, it's too much.'

'It's pocket change for me.'

'La di dah, Reid. Stop throwing your money in my face. I don't want to be your little charity project that you check in on from time to time out of the goodness of your *noblesse oblige*.' Why had Gert put those words in her head? 'I would love for you to see me as your equal—for us to meet as equals—but I'm not. I never will have your kind of generational wealth or the status you enjoy. I really liked it in the tent when money and status meant nothing, and you needed my help. I had value—I think that makes me a terrible person that you needed to be practically dying for me to consider myself of value to you, but there you have it. I really liked the way we connected, and I still do like…you. I put that under reasons *not* to contact you.'

He leaned forward, elbows on walnut inlay, and steepled his hands. 'That makes no sense.'

She wished she could see his eyes. 'Yes, it does. Self-protection. Why fall for the unobtainable when I can avoid you instead? My reasoning is sound.'

'I'm not unobtainable. I'm right here.'

Yep, right there being deliberately wilful.

'Within reach,' he added helpfully. 'Looking for a woman who's brave and resourceful and who knows this land as well as I do and who won't drive me crazy. Big bonus points if she doesn't want me for my money or status. Sound like anyone you know?'

'No.'

'Now you're just being wilful.'

'Me?' He could talk!

He took off his sunglasses, possibly so she could quiver beneath his narrowed glare. 'I dreamed about meeting you again. This isn't how it went. There was touching—lots of touching and bonding. Definitely no arguing.'

'Hey, I have great dreams too,' she murmured dulcetly. 'And then I wake up.'

He blew out a breath and got to his feet. It didn't escape her notice that he favoured one leg. 'I think I know what the problem is.' He walked to the door and turned off the light, plunging them into near darkness again. 'Much better.'

'How is this better?' Every nerve-ending she owned was waiting for his next move, his next breath. 'You can't just wish our differences away with the flick of a switch. It doesn't work like that.'

'Plenty of people think it does.' He stayed leaning with his back to the door, watching her, a grey cat in the dark. 'Let's experiment. Nothing too difficult or time-consuming, you have my word. I just want some clarity about what really went down in the dust storm.'

She was beginning to see why he was so successful in business. 'You mean besides your test helicopter?'

'I do like to run tests,' he murmured.

She got to her feet and eyed him warily. 'If I

asked you to step aside and let me leave, would you do it?'

'Of course.'

But she didn't ask and he didn't move. A curse on her curiosity. 'What kind of experiment?'

'A kiss in the dark.'

CHAPTER SEVEN

IN ARI'S EXPERIENCE, kisses were careful things, sparingly given. She was the product of a night of passion, raised by a single mother who trusted too easily, *loved* too willingly and time and time again had paid the price. Impressionable Ari had grown up wary. She wasn't against love, or trust, but they had to be earned.

'You're playing with me.' That was what play-boys did.

'I'm not.'

'You're a playboy, and rich, and you can have anyone you want. So why me?'

'I'm not a playboy. I never have been, no matter what the tabloids say. I am smart enough to know when I'm onto a good thing. We found something in that tent.' He hadn't moved. 'I want to explore it.'

'What if it's gone?'

'It hasn't. Kissing you will prove it. It's a test. I'm an engineer. Engineers love tests.' He nodded, and the light from the window caused his previously shadowed eyes to glint. 'It makes perfect sense.'

She didn't know what to make of any of it.

Her gaze dipped from his eyes to his lips, with their strong lines and tempting shape, and she wondered what it would feel like to trace them with her fingertips, taste him on her tongue. No point denying that she was tempted.

'One—' She cleared her throat and tried again. 'One kiss and if it's not…right, that's the end of it.'

'Agreed.'

Honey smooth.

Too smooth as he touched a finger beneath her chin and with the gentlest pressure tilted her head upwards. Ari clenched her hands to fists and held them rigidly at her sides so she wouldn't reach for him if the kiss did measure up to impossible expectations.

'I don't know what you think is going to hap—' But the rest of the word had nowhere to go as his lips claimed hers and set off a cascade of sensation that lit her from within. That connection she'd imagined in the tent? It was there in his kiss. A warm blaze that promised home, with teasing hints of laughter and passion licking at the edges of her thoughts.

He reached for her, broad palms against her

shoulders until he ran his hands down her arms and caught at her fists with warm fingers, teasing them open and bringing them to his chest to where his heart beat strong and sure. As the kissing continued, inviting her on a journey so full of promise she trembled with the need to take another step.

Deeper now, as her tongue tangled with his and he pulled her body closer to his, and she did nothing to discourage him. She loved the feel of being in his arms and pressed into his long, lean length and the way he savoured her as if they had all the time in the world.

It ended with a hushed quiet, his hands cradling her head and his forehead resting against hers as they traded ragged breaths and fiercely beating hearts.

And even though she didn't believe in love at first kiss, she was now a very firm believer in the lightning-bolt power of a first kiss.

'So.' She stepped away from all that hard-muscled warmth.

'So.' He sounded deeply, smugly satisfied.

'If I take up with you, chances are I'll end up with nothing. I have exams. A future I'm working hard for. I can't just…stop…because your kisses turn the world upside down.' Words spoken more for her benefit than his. 'I need to get back to work.'

'You really don't need to go back to work to-night, but I'm prepared to do this your way.' He moved aside and opened the door and bathed her in light from the hallway while he remained in the shadows. 'When do you finish your exams?'

'The nineteenth.'

'And the time?'

'Four p.m. Would you like to know where?' She could always put her snarky response down to sarcasm rather than a burning desire to set eyes on him again.

'Would you like a kiss for luck?' he asked.

'Best not. We could be here all night.' She was nervous now, because she truly had thought a kiss would put an end to his pursuit. She had nothing a man like him could possibly want. He'd been curious about the woman who'd kept him alive in the dust storm, that was all. And now that he'd found her he'd lose interest in her fast. 'I'm glad you've made such a good recovery. You deserve to soar.'

He smiled, slow and sure. 'See you 'round, Ari.'

'We'll see.' She wasn't part of his world at all. If he wanted to see her again, he'd have to come slumming in hers. 'I have to go to work.'

Ari scribbled down an answer she knew was wrong and set her pen down as the buzzer sounded. Her practical exam had involved classifying live plants, and while some had been familiar, others she'd only ever seen before in photos and botanical drawings. Growing up on the edge of channel country had given her a limited set of plants to know by heart. The rest she'd had to learn. Even her regular walks through Brisbane's botanic gardens hadn't given her the reach she'd needed for this exam.

She gathered up her exam booklets, made sure she'd written her name and student number on the top of each, and handed them to the supervisor with a sickly grimace. She might scrape through. Just. And if she didn't, it wasn't the end of the world. She'd just take the course again.

Ari breathed in through her nose and out through her mouth as she left the exam hall, hoping that the afternoon sunshine and a lung full of fresh air would help chase her grim thoughts away. Sarah, her plant classification partner, fell into step with her. 'How'd you go?' the younger woman asked.

'Touch and go.' No point pretending otherwise.

'A bunch of us are heading for the campus bar if you want to come too?'

Unlike Ari, Sarah lived on campus and was doing a degree course in horticulture full time. Sarah had study buddies and college tutors and friends to lean on. She'd been partnered with Ari for the practical component of two subjects on account of her last name being Collins. Cohen and Collins. Sarah had always gone above and beyond in her efforts to make Ari feel included, not just during coursework but within Sarah's friendship groups too.

It wasn't Sarah's fault that Ari had the social skills of a wary echidna. 'Thanks for the invite, but I'm just going to go and lick my wounds in private.'

'You sure?' They took the stairs together, in sync enough to reach the bottom at the same time. They stopped at the point the footpath split in two directions. The downward path led to the colleges. The upward path led to the car park. 'If you've passed all your other subjects with good averages and for some reason bomb this one, you can put in for special consideration,' Sarah continued.

'Good to know.'

'You sure you don't want to join us?'

'Yeah, I'm too old for all your partying ways.'

'You're, like, two years older than me!'

'Still not drinking with you, lovely.' They shuffled to the side of the paths so other students could walk past. 'Let's stay in touch, okay?'

'Yes!' Sarah beamed and hugged her for good measure. 'I have your number. Don't ghost me.'

'Go. Be merry. I promise I'll keep in touch.'

Ari didn't want to confess what she was holding out for this evening.

A long shot.

The promise of a kiss and a gravelly, *See you 'round.*

A fairy tale.

Reid leaned against the bull bar of Ari's battered old ute and waited for her to walk closer. She'd seen him from a distance—he'd noted the hitch in her step and the way she'd clutched the strap of her satchel tighter. She'd put her head down, her dark wavy hair swinging forward to partially cover her face, but she'd kept coming his way.

Granted, he'd planted himself right in her way but needs must.

He'd left her alone so she could study without distraction.

He'd found out everything he could about her.

He knew she had a stepfather and a younger stepbrother living in a house her mother had bought with cash twenty-five years ago. He knew from Gert that Ari wasn't welcome in her childhood home any more and that whenever she returned to Barcoo, the small Outback town she'd grown up in, she stayed with Gert.

No known father, dead mother, and yet somehow Ari had clung to the notion that if she worked and studied hard enough, she could make her own way.

Stubborn, resilient, driven, independent. She'd resisted his money, his gratitude, and made light of his kisses. She didn't want his help, even though it would give her a leg-up when it came to realising her dreams and securing financial independence. She didn't trust other people not to take away everything she'd strived for—he thought that might be one of the reasons she'd pushed him away, but when he pumped Gert for more information on Ari's upbringing, the older woman would only say so much. Ari's mother had married a bad 'un who'd chipped away at her confidence and self-respect until she was a shell of the woman she'd once been. Ari had copped the lash of her stepfather's belt and had the internal and external scars to prove it. Love had been scarce and trust non-existent. Gert had warned him against hurting Ari and he'd promised he wouldn't.

He wanted to make her life's journey *easier*.

Playboy, the media called him. Younger brother to dangerous, brooding, ex-con billionaire Judah Blake. Second son of a titled aristocrat—the feckless, charming spare, and once upon a time he'd done his very best to live up to that reputation.

He was the one who'd laughed and splashed his cash while beautiful women smiled prettily.

He was the one who'd wryly introduced those same women to unmarried billionaires and barons who were higher up the food chain than him. He'd crossed them off his *maybe* list as he'd watched them make their plays.

He'd met Jenna and thought she might be different. She hadn't wanted his money, she'd wanted his might, his reputation, his goals to align with hers, and when they hadn't she'd set out to destroy him.

He'd become even more jaded about relationships after that. He rarely trusted others to do right by him.

But this woman… Ari.

Maybe he could trust this one and in doing so get her to trust him. They already had a solid foundation—forged in a dust storm in a tent.

'I got your landscape plans for the eco lodges,' he said as she came to a halt in front of him. He would have searched her eyes for any sign of welcome if his eyesight had allowed for it, but she wasn't close enough for that and broad brushstrokes were all he had to work with. 'You added water.'

'I did.'

'It'll bring the wildlife and scare city people stupid.'

There was a smile, even if it happened to be a small one. 'You said the lodges were for scientists and ecologists. Surely they'll cope.'

'You'd think. Experience suggests otherwise.'

'Then don't use the plans.'

'I was thinking more along the lines of revise and resubmit.' She was in a mood and he couldn't tell if he was the reason for it, showing up like this uninvited. But he was an excellent mood-booster, and if that was to be his role this evening so be it.

When he'd been younger, he'd often had to coax his sister-in-law, Bridie, out of her house. And Gert could be curt, but Reid had always been able to get her laughing.

'How did your exam go?' he asked. Maybe that was the problem. Maybe she needed to unload, in which case he could lend an ear.

She shrugged, and her perfect mouth turned down. 'Terrible.'

Okay. 'Care to share?'

'I really don't want to talk about it.'

There went his opportunity to showcase his masterful listening skills.

'So what do you want to do this evening? Because I'm here to make it happen.'

It wasn't as if silver-spoon billionaire Reid, with his genius IQ and revolutionary engine designs, would have any experience with failure. And even if she *was* underestimating his imagination, she still didn't want to talk about her exam. 'You came.'

'I said I would. I'm a man of my word.'

Also way too easy on the eye, in his moleskin trousers and polished leather boots. He wore a collared chambray shirt, frayed at the neck, with the sleeves rolled to his elbows. He wore his battered Akubra hat with the arrogance of long familiarity. He knew who he was.

For some people, that came easily.

His smile came easily too. 'Celebrate with me tonight. You finished your course. That's a big deal.'

'Not in your world.'

He pushed his hat back and now she could see his eyes more clearly. Hazel-green with a scar that cut one eyebrow in two and ran in shredded ribbons towards his hairline. 'I live here in Brisbane for part of each year. I'd like to show you my world here if you want to see it. But there is a catch. I need to get a lift back to my place with you.' He gestured towards his eyes. 'I can't drive. They're not ready yet.'

'Will they ever be?'

He shrugged and his engaging smile turned wry. 'No one knows. My eyesight's still in flux. I'm taking that as a win, and if it stops short of where I want it to be, at least I have the resources to work around it. But enough about that. Haven't you ever wanted to have dinner with a slightly damaged billionaire? We could do the whole *Pretty Woman* playlist.'

'You mean you flash your credit card around while buying me clothes, arrange for me to wear stunning jewels, take me to all the special places and then your friends call me a whore?'

'We could cut some of that out,' he assured her. 'I can't play the piano. And I'm not afraid of heights. That guy was a mess. Daddy issues.'

'Don't you have daddy issues too?'

'Nah. My father was a gambler and apparently a womaniser, although I never saw the womaniser part until after my mother died, when he went off the rails. I put it down to grief. When she was alive, my father treated my mother like the princess she was. Displays of affection between them were rarer than dolphins in the desert, now I come to think of it, but I chalked it up to aristocratic reserve.'

'You don't seem to have much. Aristocratic reserve, I mean.' Oh, hell. Was that an insult? 'I didn't mean that as an insult.'

He smiled. 'Thanks for clarifying. I won't take it as one.'

She'd never realised just how sexy confidence could be. 'Any luck finding your half-sister?'

'Not yet. Plenty of charlatans though. We did turn up something interesting. My father gave your mother a lump sum of cash around about the time you were born.'

Ari opened her mouth to reply, and then shut it again so she wouldn't catch a fly. She felt hot then cold. She didn't *want* to be the missing Blake heiress. The thought of Reid being her half-brother made her feel ill.

She'd *kissed* him.

With feelings unbecoming to a sibling. 'My father was a stockman from the north.'

'That's what Gert says. She says she and your mother were housekeeping at Jeddah Creek station for a party of half a dozen high rollers—this was years ago—and my father was losing badly. He was about to bet Jeddah Creek station in its entirety when your mother fell to the ground while pouring them all more drinks. She told them her water just broke. It hadn't. You didn't arrive for another two weeks, according to Gert, but it did get my father away from the gambling table long enough to come to his senses. Your mother told him she'd overheard his guests discussing winning strategies. They were all in it together—against him.'

'Nasty.'

'He asked her what she wanted by way of thanks and she said, "Security for my baby." So he gave her enough money to buy a house. That's one story, anyway. I have others if you want to hear them. None of them suggest that we're related.'

'That's a relief.'

'You don't want to be the missing Blake heiress?'

'No. All the no.'

'We're not that bad.'

'We *kissed*.'

'There is that,' he murmured. 'Having to conjure up brotherly feelings for you would be difficult, given our smouldering connection.'

'It's not smouldering.'

'Incendiary?' He brightened. 'Explosive?'

'*Reid.*'

'Don't you want to hear the other stories about why my father gave your mother two hundred and fifty thousand dollars twenty-three years ago? I think you do.'

'I hope you don't want that money back. I don't have it.'

'Yeah, I heard that too.'

She didn't *like* that he seemed to know so much about her life. Had he asked around? Had Gert opened up to him about Ari's stepfather and stepbrother situation? Because, honestly, she didn't care any more that they'd turned their backs on her the moment her mother was cold. Even her mother had pushed Ari away towards the end as a way of keeping them happy. She'd never felt so alone and if it hadn't been for Gert stepping in and offering her a home, Ari didn't know what she would have done. She'd stopped thinking of them as family years ago. She was doing all right on her own these days, thank you very much, and she dared anyone to think otherwise.

'So that's your ticked-off look,' he mused. 'I wish I could see it better.'

'Do you? *Do you really?*'

'And I really like your *dire warning* voice. I promise I'll behave.'

'Are you always this jokey?'

'You're in a mood. I'm trying to cajole you out of it. I'm offering you the mood-lifting Cinderella experience. And all you have to do to get it started is give me a lift and your company for the evening.'

With a sigh that was more for show than for protest, she gave in. He'd already managed to take her mind off her study failures. His mood-boosting skills actually were as good as advertised. And there was also the not so small effort it had taken him to arrange to be waiting for her.

She'd told him about liking their time in the tent because she felt useful, and here he was throwing himself on her mercy for a lift and ceding control. *Journey with me,* he might as well have said. *You drive. I trust you.* She'd never even *seen* a relationship dynamic like the one he seemed to be offering her. Did he realise how paper-thin her defences against him were? 'I'll do it. On one condition.'

'Name it.'

'Please don't dress me up and take me to the opera this evening. Or to a ball. Or to a fancy dinner with the flying snails and challenging silverware. Can we give that a miss?'

'As you wish.'

She headed for the driver's side door. 'How'd you get here?'

'Uber.'

'And how'd you know this was my car?'

'Gert said you drove a thirty-year-old Hilux. This one has red dust in its wheel rims. Calculated guess.'

'I wish there'd been more of those in my exam.' She blew out a breath. She wasn't going to think about that. Nothing she could do about it. 'My passenger-side door isn't locked. Jump in.'

He reached for the passenger-door handle. 'You don't lock it?'

'Who'd want it? Besides, the locks have been broken for years. I also need to drive us to the nearest mechanic. I was almost late for my exam because Bessie wouldn't start. I think it's the battery.' She didn't want to think about all the other things it could be.

She'd parked on an incline with the nose facing downhill and no other cars in front of her, and after two sluggish attempts at getting the engine to turn over, she blew out a breath, shoved the vehicle in neutral, released the brake and let it roll until she could clutch-start the beast.

It started with a jolt and she found second gear with barely a grind and then they were on their way. 'Atta girl.' She patted the dash.

'That is so sexy,' he murmured. 'Can you muster cattle too? Fix a broken five-wire fence?'

'Is that what turns you on?'

'It's never been a complete turn-on before. I'd have found it interesting but not necessarily a reason to pursue a woman. Maybe it's just you.'

No getting past his open interest in pursuing her. She was simultaneously grateful for his clarity and sure that his pursuit would be short-lived. 'You know what I'm going to do for you? I'm going to save us a lot of trouble and show you the real me.'

'I can't wait. How else are we going to get to know each other?' he murmured agreeably as they reached a stop sign and Ari prayed the ute didn't stall. 'What did you have planned for this evening before I turned up?'

'You mean after the trip to the mechanic? If I only had to buy a new battery, I was thinking I'd go home, get Thai takeaway from the restaurant down the road, put some music on and open a bottle of beer. Because that's how I roll.' She had her eyes on the road and couldn't see his reaction to her big night of celebration. 'There may have been a little singalong and a toast to me for sticking to my education plan in the face of poverty. You're welcome to join me. I'm not wedded to the Cinderella plan.' They'd hit the main road. 'Can you bring up directions to the nearest battery place?'

'I have a better idea.'

Ten minutes later, Reid had directed her to a workshop of some kind on the outskirts of Fortitude Valley near Brisbane city centre. Huge industrial doors stood open and Ari could see several vehicles inside.

'Drive in. Bay three should be free.'

'What is this place?'

'It's where my team converts regular vehicles to electric ones.'

'Uh-huh.'

'Don't worry.' He'd caught her sideways glance. 'Converting this old dear is out of the question. Probably. But they're all mechanics or engineers of some kind and they can give it a once-over and get it running properly for you.'

She found bay three and parked as requested. By the time she'd collected her shoulder bag, Reid was already out and talking with a dark-haired man with grey streaks through his beard.

Both men turned towards her as they approached. 'Stan, meet Ari. Ari, this is Stan. He vets my engine designs and tells me I'm dreaming.'

'Sounds about right.' Stan nodded. 'Cheers. We'll take a look at the old girl and give you a call when she's ready. Meanwhile, we've got a replacement ride for you. Special order for Reid, here. Even better if you get to be the test driver while he's in it.'

'Told you I had a good idea,' he murmured.

Stan led them to what looked like a brand-new farm four-wheel-drive. 'Hybrid fuel, double cab manual workmate with a cab chassis, bull bar, front winch, towbar, lockbox, air pump in the lockbox, off-road tyres, and an air intake upgrade.' Stan patted the hood. 'Outback baby, as requested.'

Reid nodded. 'Torque?'

'Four hundred Nm max. Best we could do.'

Ari had no idea what they were talking about but nodded along with them, only to find two sets of eyes on her, expressing no little amusement.

'What? I can admire an Outback baby when I see one. Long as it gets me where I'm going.'

'Good, because I had it tricked out especially for you.' Reid opened the driver's-side door for her. 'Even if I haven't figured out a way to make you accept it. Yet.'

CHAPTER EIGHT

ARI TOSSED HER bag on the seat, grabbed the handhold and hoisted herself up. How was she supposed to object to his gifting her this beautiful Outback vehicle when he hadn't even tried to give it to her? Yet.

Reid stayed where he was, arms crossed in front of him. 'You want a running board on this thing?'

'I'm only driving it for one evening, no matter what you think the future holds.'

'Maybe just a running *step*,' he mused. 'You're still going to need the clearance.'

'We are not even having the same conversation.' She took the time to absorb that new car smell and all the bells and whistles—phone slot, big screen. 'This thing isn't going to take over the driving, is it?'

'Not if you don't want it to—although I think the boys did add self-drive capabilities. Needs testing in the desert, though.'

'Huh. Another prototype?'

'This is me you're talking to. Everything that comes out of this workshop is a prototype.'

Hopefully not as life-challenging as his last one.

The truck was ridiculously easy to drive, and comfortable as well. Windows that sealed—no whistling wind. A dash that didn't rattle. No leaves fluttering in the broken air-conditioning vent. This air conditioning actually *worked*.

The air conditioning alone was enough to make her high-falutin' principles waver.

'How's it drive?'

'I feel like a princess in a golden carriage. Good job.'

Even the dratted man's quiet laughter made her feel happy. What was it about him that made her want to sign up for so much more?

But the car beeped whenever she got too close to other vehicles, and basically critiqued her driving the entire way to the inner-city warehouse apartment complex that Reid programmed into the car's computer.

'Okay, I'm over the helpful driving suggestions and my admiration for functioning air conditioning,' she said as she turned the vehicle into an underground car park with a rolling security door that slid open at the press of his keychain.

'You can keep the carriage, I'd like my old one back at midnight, please. Where are we?'

'Hamilton. I live here when I'm in Brisbane. A lot of my tech guys live here too—it's part of their wage package. There's a shopping strip across the road with a couple of clothing boutiques, restaurants and a bar.'

'Does that mean you own the whole woolshed apartment complex and the shopping strip too?'

His silence gave her a jolt. 'Oh. Hell. You do. I can't even—' She owned so little. 'We are so different.'

'Not that different,' he murmured. 'I aim to prove it to you. Park near the lift.'

She did.

The step down from the cab of the vehicle really was a bit steep for her, but she wasn't about to complain. Cinderella would have had a terrible time getting in and out of her carriage, would she not? In that gown?

She met up with Reid at the back of the vehicle but instead of leading her to the lift, he headed for the car-park entrance.

'So, we're heading for my place and takeaway and beer,' he told her, 'but there's water involved, which I think you'll like, and one of the boutiques across the road does swimwear and leisure wear. My shout for the swimwear and whatever you want to wear tonight. All part of the Cinderella deal. Payment, if you like, for holding my hand and tormenting me with your plant classification textbook.'

'I was *studying*.'

'I was barely conscious and unable to protest!'

Well, there was that. 'Sorry. I was trying to take your mind—and mine—off our situation. Which was *dire*.'

He had such a rich, rumbling laugh. 'Exactly. And you rose to the challenge magnificently, so whatever you want from the boutique is on me. Or you can swim naked. I wouldn't object.'

Or she might not swim at all. A far more likely option to her way of thinking.

But she walked with him to the swimwear boutique with its skinny mannequins and beach towels in the window, and Ari just knew by looking at the shop's high-end styling that the prices would be out of her reach. Who could afford hundreds of dollars for tiny brightly coloured bits of material, not to mention hundreds more for the various wraps and skirts that went with them? She headed for the specials rack. Reid headed for the counter and the smiling, sun-kissed woman behind it.

'Reid Blake. Fancy seeing you here,' the woman said, and her voice was warmly caressing but somehow not predatory.

'Rita.' He leaned against the counter. 'This is

Ari. I've hijacked her evening, and she now needs a swimsuit and loungewear.'

'That I'm paying for, no matter what he says, so I'll be over here by the specials rack,' said Ari.

Reid sighed. 'See what I'm dealing with here, Rita? Insubordination. Help me.'

Rita looked aghast as she floated towards the specials rack. 'But Ari, darling, it's been a long day with very few customers. My commission is begging you to let him pick up the tab. He never comes in here flashing his big black credit card. The bike shop, sure. The Thai restaurant next door, often. Here, never.'

'Uh-huh.' Ari didn't believe a word of the woman's patter. He was probably in here every other week.

'Ari,' the woman said quietly, with a brief glance towards Reid. 'Not once.'

Ari didn't know what to do with that information.

'Reid, go order us some of those yummy little spring rolls from next door, while I open the champagne,' commanded Rita. 'Make yourself scarce. We're busy.'

'Rita's my next-door neighbour.' Reid fished a black plastic card from his wallet and set it on the counter with a snap. 'Ari is Cinderella tonight. You are her fairy godmother. We're going swimming later, and if you charge her for any of the clothes she selects I will double your rent.' He tapped the card. 'Got it?'

'Loud and clear, Your Lordshipness,' said Rita with a dismissive wave. 'Leave us.'

He left with swagger that Rita admired, right up until the door closed behind him, and then the older woman snorted, and Ari couldn't help but smile right along with her.

'That man.' Rita walked to the door and flipped a 'Closed' sign outwards. 'He tries so hard to be a hard ass but it never sticks. He's a country boy with a lot of money and a burning desire to improve the lives of everyone around him. But I am telling the truth that he's never spent in here before. You must be special.'

'No.' Never special. 'I'm just...someone from home. Where he grew up.'

'Sounds special enough to me. One piece or two for swimwear?'

'Two? Or... I don't know. I don't swim much. I'm kind of a get-wet-up-to-my-middle if it's the ocean and an edge-clinger if it's a pool.'

'Trust me, he's not going to let you drown. I'm thinking a two-piece with a bespoke silk wrap and matching skirt. Coral reef colours with a bit of blue and seafoam. Trust me, I'm your fairy godmother and that there's a centurion credit card he's left on my counter. He can afford the designer silk.'

'But I don't want him to pay.'

Rita disappeared behind a curtain and returned with an armful of seafoam silk glory.

'Oh. That looks like nightwear.'

'Well, it is five p.m.' Rita held up the swimwear. 'You're a neat size ten and this will fit you to perfection. Try it on.'

'No.'

Which Rita somehow interpreted as *I'll take it.*

'The skirt is a wraparound—one size fits all. The wrap is gorgeous—so sheer, and there's a camisole and panties to go with it as well as a swimsuit. It's a honeymoon combo. From champagne and strawberries and ruffled sheets to a quick dip in the spa to soothe those aching muscles, it's got you covered, so to speak.'

'None of it look like it's going to cover very *much.*'

'Oh, sweetheart. You be you. I'll open the champagne, and then we can really get started. We can cover more of you if that's what you'd prefer.'

Was champagne a thing on a Friday afternoon in a closed swimwear shop? Apparently, it was, and there were triple Brie cheese and fig jam and salted crackers too. By the time Reid returned, Rita had added pleated long trousers, a beaded silk sleeveless top, and pretty leather sandals to Ari's pile.

Reid had returned with enough finger food for ten people, and out came plates and forks and a guy dropped in with a big jug of beer and stayed for a satay stick with peanut chilli sauce and was this a bizarre way to spend a Friday evening in the river city? It didn't seem all that billionaireish.

Instead, Ari got to laugh as Rita and brew master Tanner, who owned the bar next door, swapped tall tales about customers and worked their way steadily through the food and beer.

By the time they left the shop and entered the old wool warehouse on the river's edge, Ari knew all about Rita's husband and one-year-old grand-daughter, and brew master Tanner's experimental passionfruit beer pop that needed finessing because it tasted—he readily admitted—really awful.

The sun had started to disappear behind tall buildings, and coloured lights were beginning to wrap the city in their glow, and Ari felt pleasure sink into her skin. She liked this city with its moist heart and sticky nights. She liked Reid's company and not just because she was two glasses of cham-pagne down and carrying a couple of thousand dol-lars' worth of almost-there clothing in two fancy recyclable carry bags. Apart from his dedication to giving her a Cinderella experience, his life and friendships seemed extraordinarily normal.

'I like your neighbourhood. And your friends. You're a people person. Who knew?'

'I knew,' said Reid as he unlocked an apart-ment door with the press of his finger on a door pad and ushered her into a soaring space with exposed brick walls and enormous glass doors at one end of the long narrow living space, lushly decorated with textured furnishings and dozens of paintings that shouldn't have worked when all piled together but they did.

Beyond the glass doors was a terrace that led to a delicately lit infinity pool that seemed to flow into the river. There was a spa section to one side, with a rock wall and spouts. Waterfall option, her brain supplied helpfully. She could picture Reid relaxing in this space. She could picture herself in it too, courtesy of the swimwear he'd just purchased for her.

'What do you think? Do you like it?'

She wanted to say something snarky about him not needing her approval. She wanted to chide him about having way too much money to spend on making his Brisbane crash pad a showstopper, but the words never left her mouth.

In truth, she didn't want to say any of that.

Why *shouldn't* he have a home full of beauty that instantly made people feel comfortable and welcome? Who was she to try and take him down with petty envy?

'I love it,' she said honestly. 'It's beautiful.'

'Guest suite is through that door to your left. My bedroom and a few other rooms are to the right, and my office takes up the mezzanine. I started this day aiming to whisk you away to an island tonight to impress you.' He walked to the big glass doors and again pressed his hand to a steel pad and the doors slid silently open until there was no visible glass wall left at all. This apartment was modest when it came to space and mighty with its bells and whistles. 'But there's water here too.' He looked back at her. 'I'm not backing out of our Cinderella deal, but we could stay here and order in and if it's beer you want, Tanner will deliver.'

'You say that as if we'd be slumming.' She couldn't figure him out. 'You have to know that my version of this evening comes nowhere near this standard of luxury. Isn't that what you want me to know?'

'Not exactly.'

She waited for him to continue.

'I want you to recognise that I get takeaway and beer and relax at home too. Just like you.'

Maybe her bedsit rental *was* the same as this place underneath. A place to cook, a place to sleep. She looked past the museum-quality paintings on the walls to the pool and spa and river and city lights on the other side of the bank.

Who was she to deny him his fantasy? 'So I go left, get changed, and meet you at the pool?'

'We could do that.' His eyes held so many smiles in them. She wondered what it would be like to be so full up with smiles that they tumbled out of her the way Reid's seemed to. Maybe if she stuck around, she'd find out. 'I'm sure you can figure out that there's a door leading from your suite onto a patio and from there you can access the pool area. You put a tent up around a severely wounded pilot in the middle of a dust storm in the desert. I'm pretty sure you can find a door.'

'You're still harping on that?' She didn't know why. 'You'd have done the same.'

'I like to think so. Doesn't make it any less impressive. I'm an awesome person. So are you.'

His confidence was contagious and he made her laugh. There were worse starts to an evening. 'Is this a date?' She needed to know. 'Or is this just you feeling beholden and thinking Ari's an awesome person?'

'It's a date. Although awesome Ari and grateful Reid are in play too. Do we need to overthink it? Because if we do, you should know that water helps. Have a problem? Have a shower. A heavy day? The spa pool is for you and don't forget to pummel your shoulders beneath the waterfall spout. I'm a believer.'

'I'm glad you don't take water for granted,' she said.

'You know where I grew up. Three-minute showers, no waiting for the water to warm up. Water is life. Which is why your designs for my eco lodges went all in on it. For you, luxury means free-flowing water available to all.' He tucked his hands into his trouser pockets. 'I came across some garden diaries written by an Outback farmer in South Australia. I bought them for you. Thirty years' worth. They're on your bed.'

Her bed?

And what a gift.

'Reid…' She didn't know what to say. *This* was what his money bought. Access to information that wasn't readily available. A step up that wasn't available to everyone. 'I don't know what to say.'

'Say you'll read them and resubmit your garden plans for my eco lodges. My north star is that we never stop learning and striving to respect the balance of nature.'

She was rapidly acquiring mad respect for this man, along with irresistible attraction, and she didn't know what to do with either. 'I'll read them. Thank you. See you in the pool.' She'd become a woman of choppy sentences. 'I'll be clinging to the edge or sitting on the step-in, if there is one.' Time to admit another of her failings. 'I can't swim.'

He took it in his stride with barely a blink. He shrugged and smiled warm and wide. 'Want to learn?'

Reid knew what women wanted him for. Access to his money and the high life, first and foremost.

His name and nebulous ties to English aristocracy came second. His personality, his beliefs and values—too many women of his acquaintance didn't care about any of that. They didn't see him and never would.

That was why Ari was special.

She saw him—the boy who'd come looking for her whenever she strayed too far from the homestead. The one she'd sat next to at the kitchen table while Gert served up reprimand along with sweet biscuits and cold water. Those memories would compete with those from the tent and now he was showing her the meat of his world and he hoped she would layer them all together and come up with someone she liked, because he sure as sunrise liked her.

She knew where he came from. Same view when they travelled Outback roads. Same sunrises and sunsets and redgums and flash-flooding rivers cutting grooves through the earth.

He could teach her to swim, to soar, if she'd let him.

If she'd lower her guard and let him in.

CHAPTER NINE

THE BIKINI SHE'D chosen seemed far smaller now than in the shop, but the colours were ones she knew well. Burnt umber, sky blue, wattle yellow and the bright red of Lilli Pilli berries.

The swimwear emphasised her slight curves and made the most of her legs. Garden work had given her lean muscle, and her wavy hair reached the small of her back. She had no gloss that came from beauty treatments and skilfully applied make-up, but what she did have going for her was her health, youth, a heart-shaped face, and good teeth. And when she slipped on the silky robe that matched her swimsuit, Ari felt almost beautiful.

It was hard not to feel special in such expensive surroundings.

Her Cinderella moment came with bare feet, an infinity pool and Reid Blake in all his near naked glory. Board shorts couldn't hide the scars that littered his body—he wasn't even trying to cover them up as he sat on the edge of the spa pool and waited for her to join him, his gaze bright and admiring as she approached.

Was she little more than a colourful shape? What did he see when he looked her way?

Why did his shortcomings embolden her?

'I usually start in the hot pool,' he said as she joined him. 'Seats and water jets are around the outside, it's deeper in the middle but you'll still be able to stand up and your head will be out of the water. All good? Feeling confident?'

'Yes.' She already loved the concept of spa baths. Now all she had to do was embrace the reality.

He eased into the water, and she shed her wrap and followed his lead and let the warm water lap at her skin.

'I've never been in one,' she confessed.

'Find a seat, rest your head against the head-rests and let go,' he suggested, and she did just that, but there was nothing to hold onto and she couldn't relax.

And then he was easing his big body into the seat alongside her and taking her hand in his at the surface of the water and it was just enough to anchor her.

'Relax,' he murmured. 'If your legs and arms want to float to the surface, let them. If you want to put your feet down and your knees up, do it.'

'I think hand-holding's our thing.' She hadn't let his hand go but she wasn't squeezing it to bits either. She closed her eyes, tilted her head back against the padded headrest and sighed her pleasure. 'This is nice. We wouldn't have got this in my bedsit. It doesn't even have a bath.'

'How are you feeling about starting your new job?'

About that…

She'd heard from the nursery manager yesterday. 'You know how Gert was bragging about me already having a job to go to? There's been a slight change of plans.'

'I'm listening.'

'The owner's son came back from overseas and is "assessing his options", whatever that means. They don't want me just yet. They may not want me at all. They're going to let me know in a couple of months' time.' She blew out a breath. 'I think I'm done with them. Goodbye, Cairns.' She released Reid's hand to remove a wayward strand of hair from her face and tuck it behind her ear. 'I'm disappointed.'

'Work for me.' The confident way he said it mixed with the heat of the water and the gently rising steam and made her light-headed. 'Better still, I'll help you lodge the paperwork to create your own company and you can work for me as a contractor.'

'You hate my garden plans for your eco lodges.'

'Hate's a strong word.'

'You're not denying it.'

'I want to give you a proper project brief this time. I want you to move into one of my lodges and live there for a month or two. There's another lodge nearby and people will come and go. Get a feel for what my visitors respond to and how they interact with their surroundings and then submit a new set of landscape plans. I'll give you a three-month contract in two stages, development and completion.'

'You're serious.'

'Very. And you can look at it as charity or pay-back for saving my life if you must. There's no denying that your remarkably brave actions are what first got my attention.'

'You think I'm brave?'

'Yes.' And not just that. 'I had grit and determination and resilience when I took on Jeddah Creek station at seventeen. The same kind of grit and resilience and determination I see in you. And back then I had help, from Tom and Bridie and Judah and others, and I took it and it set me up for a future I never dreamed of.'

He wasn't finished.

'I don't want to take anything from you. I don't want to deny you the chance to work and grow and travel in directions you've never dreamed of. I want you to have help too, like I did. I want to pay it forward. I want to see you soar.'

Did she dare believe him? Trust him to do right by her?

Could she trust her own instincts when what he was offering sounded too good to be true?

He leaned back and closed his eyes, possibly to avoid her open-mouthed disbelief as she scrambled to sit upright. He'd left her with no defence against his generosity. 'Say yes.'

It was a chance in a million. 'You want to see me succeed?'

'Absolutely.'

'No strings attached? Regardless of whether I end up in your bed tonight?'

He lifted his head and studied her through narrowed eyes. 'I'm ruling that out for now. I'm playing the long game. But even if we do get romantically involved, my offer will stand. I want you to create a work future you're passionate about.'

He speared through the water to the opposite corner of the spa pool and turned to face her with the arc of an eyebrow. 'Say yes to the contract.'

Gert had vouched for him.

It really was the opportunity of a lifetime. 'What happens if we have a *very intense, very short-lived* affair and discover we're not that compatible after all?'

'You'll still have a company that has nothing to do with me and a lucrative, high-impact landscape-gardening project under way or completed. Your work will speak for itself, and you'll have other projects lined up, none of them connected to me.' His quiet words carried across the sound of bubbling warm water. 'I'm trying to empower you, Ari. Place you in a position where, no matter what happens, you win.'

'Even if you lose?'

'I'll have had my chance with you and taken my shot. How is that losing?'

Did he have no fear at all? What if he lost his heart to her and she trampled on it? What was he *seeing* when he gazed at her so steadily? 'Aren't you scared of giving your heart to the wrong person?'

'You and I, we have a lot in common. We don't trust easily. Stands out a mile. People have let us down. Which means that one of us has to blink first and say I trust you and I want you and I'm ready for whatever that brings. I don't think you'll let me down, and I sure as hell won't let you down. It's a good start to whatever kind of relationship we forge, don't you think?'

Could she really walk away from Reid's captivating confidence?

No.

No, she could not. 'I'll work my butt off until you're happy with my work. Like that blasted exam, I'll do it over and over until I get it right. I won't let you down.'

'I know you won't.'

'And we probably shouldn't ruin my golden opportunity with…y'know…sex right now. Too soon. Like you said.' *But, oh, how she wanted to ruin it.* 'That's very chivalrous of you.'

'Long game, remember?' And then he was looking straight at her, with a glint of challenge in his eyes. 'Swimming lesson number one. Push off the edge of the seat section with your feet, arms out in front of you and let your body glide through the water towards me. I'll catch you.'

'But it's all bubbly in the middle.'

'So it'll tickle. Believe me, your body can do it. Don't overthink it. Push off and glide. Believe.'

It was so *easy* to believe around him.

Moments later her hands hit his chest and she tried very hard not to scramble for purchase and cling to him like a vine. She found her feet and blushed as she snatched her hands away. 'You just wanted my hands on your hot bod.'

'Former hot bod,' he countered dryly. But you're right in thinking I like your hands on me. 'Now turn around and push off again and glide back to the other side. Don't put your feet down until your hands touch the wall.'

Pretty soon she was gliding all over the place while Reid drawled lazy suggestions to go faster, slower, and change direction midway across without putting her feet down.

'Taking control is addictive,' he said at last, when she'd settled into her spa seat with a great deal more confidence than she'd had to begin with. 'Whether it's taking control of something you're doing, or directing others, it can be a buzz. After a while it becomes second nature, and you start to think you know more and make better choices than anyone else. It's rubbish, of course, but no one tells you that to your face because you're the boss with the endless line of credit. Eventually that way of thinking bleeds into every part of your life, romance included.'

'So you're...bossy in bed?'

'Would you like me to be?' He had a wicked grin.

She eased lower, up to her chin in bubbly water because maybe then he wouldn't see the blush that felt as if it went all the way from her cheeks to her chest.

'I like teasing you,' he said next. 'You take the bait so beautifully.'

She retaliated by splashing water in his face, and she really should have thought that through because moments later they were both splashing each other for all they were worth, as if they were twelve.

Fifteen at the most.

It ended with a drenching and Reid pinning her against the side of the pool, with his arms beneath her shoulders, holding her up, and her body bumping against his and finding all sorts of interesting developments.

'You see, this is what I *don't* get from the women I date,' he murmured.

'Told off?'

'Scolded. Taken to task. Given a tongue-lashing,' he added.

'Are you *sure* you don't get that last one?'

'Cinderella!' He sounded delighted. 'You're *raunchy*. Bawdy. Risqué. I love it.'

'Cinderella was not raised a lady, Reid. Do keep up with your fairy tales.'

'I have to kiss you.'

He had quite the flair for drama, or was it silliness? She loved it. 'Because you're unbearably smitten?'

He angled closer until their lips were almost touching and she didn't pull away. 'Mainly to shut you up,' he murmured, and then his lips were on hers, cool and sure, tempting and teasing until she opened for him and let the heat take hold.

It wasn't like their last kiss. He didn't see the need to ask more wordless questions he already knew the answer to. He turned playfulness into searing desire so fast she was in danger of drowning.

Ari clung to him, her heart tight in her chest as his hands caressed her skin, wove through her hair and he cradled her close.

He'd been living rent-free in her head for so many weeks now, but the reality of being in his company again was so much better than anything she'd imagined, and she'd imagined a lot.

Water had long been one of her favourite things. Reid was fast becoming her favourite person. Put the two together and she had no defences left.

Ari didn't end the kiss, Reid did.

He took a step back, leaving her clinging to the pool edge as he ran not quite steady hands through his already soaked hair.

'Think I need a cool-down,' he murmured, and turned and climbed from the hot pool and entered the larger lap pool. Sexy guy. Even with his carved-up leg and visible injuries.

Sexy guy who wanted her, Ari Cohen—nothing special—in his life and was going to quite some lengths to make it happen.

Which in Ari's opinion made him *even* more desirable.

She rested her forearms on the side of the spa and watched as he swam a couple of laps, his movements slow and precise. Still recovering, her brain supplied helpfully.

'You're a pretty good date,' she said when he surfaced at the side closest to her and didn't attempt another lap. 'More of a fairy godmother than Prince Charming, though.'

'I'll take it under advisement.'

He left the pool and reached for a towel from a pile sitting on a small side table. He scrubbed his face and hair dry and wrapped the towel around his waist. When she made her own exit from the water, he handed her a towel too.

'It's a lot to take in.' She didn't look at him as she dried off and reached for her pretty silk wrap. 'I've never thought much beyond having to take care of myself. There's never been a Prince Charming on my horizon until you dropped from the sky.'

'I thought you said I was the fairy godmother.'

'Yeah, well, maybe you're both.' She wanted to make another confession, so he would know all her limitations up front. 'I've never been in a relationship. Never even tried to trust a man to put my well-being on equal par with his. I didn't exactly have good role models for that.' She was looking for a reaction from him, but he didn't flinch. 'I've had sex. No strings. One-offs. They fit my sense of self-worth.'

'Work on that,' he commanded gruffly.

'I will. I am. You're helping with that by offering me options I've never dreamed of, and it's a lot. *You're* a lot to take on, this world you inhabit isn't one I've lived in, even though you're doing your best to make it seem mostly normal. For me it's a lot, so thanks for taking it slow.'

'All part of my plan for world domination, but you're welcome.' He'd finished towelling his hair dry and it stuck up in tufts, going every which way. 'How about we have that beer now? Or food. You hungry? There's a riverfront restaurant a short walk from here if you feel like dining out. Or we can have it delivered. Your call.'

She had wet hair, no make-up, and beautiful casual clothes to change into. She didn't want to add anyone else to the night's mix. 'I'd like to hang around here and eat in. We could put together that design brief you mentioned earlier. I could cover your gorgeous outdoor table in scribbled notes and drawings while you describe what you want to achieve. There could be half-eaten plates of food and boutique beer on the table that no one's rushing to clear away. And maybe at the end of the evening as I'm walking out the door to catch a ride home, there could be farewell kissing and a promise to catch up again soon.'

'That's your wish for the evening?'

'Yeah.' Pretty simple. And yet every moment of it had the potential to make her heart sing. 'Too lame?'

'Not at all.'

The evening unfolded with a magic born of stunningly beautiful surroundings, the prioritising of creativity, imagination, and the feeding of the senses.

Not to mention the teasing, flirting and touching.

When Reid finally walked her to the Cinderella truck that he insisted she drive home, there were plans afoot for her new landscape-design company and for her to take up residence in one of the Cooper's Creek station lodges from next week onwards.

Whatever this was that flowed back and forth between them like gossamer strands of an ever-growing spiderweb, she'd surrendered to it.

She would shelve her defences and see where it led and maybe *that* was the greatest takeaway gift of the evening.

Not the pretty clothes or the access to information, but her willingness to believe in possibilities of her own making. With a little help from a friend.

CHAPTER TEN

A WEEK LATER, with the contents of her bedsit sold to strangers and her more prized possessions stored at Gert's place, Ari set out for her new accommodation. She had her faithful old ute back in her possession and it was running better than ever on account of its new engine, new tyres, and some kind of satellite link that had been added to the dash. The satellite technology gave her GPS, Internet and music, no matter which direction she travelled or how remote her destination.

It was amazing.

When she'd wanted to pay for the upgrades, Reid had waved her offer away with a steely glare. When she'd broached the subject of paying rent, he'd countered with, 'I broke your tent, now you get to use my accommodation. It's a fair exchange. Besides, there's a brown boronia, a Sturt's desert pea, and half a dozen grafted grevilleas waiting for you at the lodge and I'm challenging you to keep them alive.'

Go with it. Just go with it. Accept the challenge and give it your best shot.

And here she was, parking her car outside the fancifully named Red Gum Lodge, given that it consisted of rammed-earth walls and a corrugated-iron roof covered in solar panels. The only timber she could see was on the north-east-facing deck, and the framing of the tall, narrow windows set deeply into the walls. The cabin would be cool inside, even with the evaporative air-conditioning unit turned off. Large concrete water tanks had been buried in the ground and the tops provided a large open area between the two lodges. The tanks had been outlined with rock walls and in the centre, the remnants of a campfire. People, yes. Vehicles, no. It was functional space, but not beautiful. The bones were there but it had been let go.

Someone had made an effort to plant trees and shrubs around the buildings, and the extensive notes Reid had given her about the original design revealed that there were greywater recycling systems in place. A quick lap around both lodges told her that water capture didn't seem to be happening.

Each apartment had two or three bedrooms, one bathroom, two toilets, and separate living, dining and kitchen areas. No open-plan beauties for this build—the architect had wanted inhabitants to be able to close off different areas of the house for better temperature control. The furnishings were high end and the colour scheme was earthy and relaxing. Gorgeous landscape photographs, taken by Reid's sister-in-law Bridie, hung on the walls, bringing the outside in.

Her apartment, a two-bedder, was the nicest place she'd ever lived in. She didn't have much to bring in and after that she stood on the deck and looked clear to the horizon as a playful wind whipped at her hair and rustled narrow leaves.

She couldn't resist stretching her arms wide and twirling in delight at her good fortune.

Even if it had come at the expense of Reid's misfortune.

The thought sobered her, and she stopped twirling and lifted her face to the sky and pleaded for Reid's well-being.

Gert had confided that Reid's latest health check hadn't brought with it the good news he'd hoped for. Ari had only spent that one evening with him in Brisbane, but towards the end of it she'd begun to get a feel for how hard he worked to make his stride look normal, his eyesight seem normal, his recovery appear complete.

It was a charade he'd kept up until the very end and it had troubled her, even if she'd chosen not to confront him about it.

Unpacking felt like coming home.

Boxes in the spare bedroom and her toiletries cluttering up the bathroom. She opened windows to take the stuffiness out of the air, and turned on the hot-water system and pump, and the air con as well. Groceries in the kitchen and her clothes in the bedroom cupboard.

Clothes that included the dazzling casual outfit Reid had bought for her, and she showered with the water still cold and slipped the top and trousers on and the pretty sandals too, before heading outside and taking a selfie with the sunset in the background, her hair whipping around her face and her smile as wide as it ever got. It was a good picture, even if it wasn't up to Bridie Starr standards.

Trusting her instincts, she sent the selfie to Reid. Maybe he could make it big on his computer screen if he couldn't see a smaller phone version.

Tease, he texted back a couple of minutes later. Settling in?

Beautiful home, she wrote back.

Moments later another message announced its arrival with a ping.

Not too isolated?

No.

Solitude had long been her friend and she had plenty to be going on with. Cairns would have been a nice change, she was sure, but this stark, unforgiving landscape was her happy place.

Thank you for the push. And for believing me.

My pleasure.

Her pleasure too.

Thank you again.

By the end of her first fortnight at Red Gum Lodge Ari had driven thousands of kilometres from one corner of Cooper's Crossing station to the next, following waterways and rocky outcrops, stock routes and wildlife corridors. She journalled wildlife sightings and plant species, and if Reid had begun to feature in her daydreams, maybe it was because she'd expected him to turn up one day, out of the blue, and he hadn't yet, and she was getting edgy.

Her 'Reid will appear like magic' scenario that she returned to every night was wishful thinking right up until the afternoon it wasn't.

She pulled up outside her lodge to find the other lodge occupied and a familiar white work truck parked alongside it.

Bridie Starr stood on the deck of the other dwelling and waved as Ari approached. Lady

Blake these days. Award-winning photographer and wife of Lord Judah Blake. Catwalk model in her teenage years, mistress of Devil's Kiss pastoral station that had now been folded into Jeddah station reserve. Between Jeddah Creek, Cooper's Crossing and Devil's Kiss, the Blake Family controlled thousands of acres of south-west Queensland. No mining, only eco-tourism, limited grazing. Conservation.

Bridie turned away from Ari as another figure joined her.

Not her husband Judah, as Ari had expected.

Reid.

Ari approached them with a skip in her step, digging deep for a confidence she was far from feeling. 'Visitors!'

'I told him you wouldn't be far away,' Bridie countered with a smile. 'We've come bearing fresh-caught barramundi, lemons, salad greens and your favourite biscuits from Gert. I was going to stay overnight, but I've been spying on a red-backed kingfisher family all week, and Judah's just spotted one of the chicks. He's swinging by to pick me up.'

'If you ask me, he can't bear to part with you overnight,' said Reid, his eyes hidden behind dark sunglasses and his gait a little stiff. He didn't attempt the trio of steps that would have brought him from the deck down to her level.

Which left her looking up at them.

'Either way, Judah's picking me up in the helicopter in half an hour,' said Bridie cheerfully. 'Ari, promise me you won't let Reid drive the truck.'

'It's self-drive,' Reid protested.

'And we know how well *that* works out here, don't we?' countered Bridie.

'It needs a little tweaking,' replied Reid, and although he didn't sound defensive he did sound kind of strained.

Not about to get in the middle of *that*, thought Ari. Although… 'Hey, Reid, if I drive you wherever you want to go while you're here, and never stop running my mouth because I haven't spoken to anyone in a week, that would be a fair exchange, right?'

'Totally fair,' Bridie answered while Reid stayed silent. 'Ari, do you want to do a walkaround while I take some *before* shots of the outdoor areas for your website?'

'My…what?'

'You can tell me what you have planned for the place. I'd love to know. I'm a silent partner in these lodges.'

'*So* far from silent…' murmured Reid.

'My design's still in the planning stages.' Ari felt compelled to explain her lack of progress. 'So far, it's been all about the plants. But good to know I don't just have Reid to impress. Who else do I need to worry about?'

'It'll come together,' said Reid, as if he refused to doubt it for a second, but she noticed his white-knuckled grip on the wooden railing of the deck, and the pinched grooves around his mouth. 'Although practise your presentation on Bridie, by all means.'

'You're not joining us?'

'Later.'

Something definitely seemed off with him, but she couldn't put her finger on it. Did he not want to be here?

Why had he come if he didn't want to be here?

And then Bridie joined her, camera in hand, and started walking and there was nothing for it but to give Reid an awkward wave and catch up with the other woman.

Ari began to outline her plans while Bridie nodded and took photos, sneaking in a couple of shots of Ari.

'Don't do me,' Ari protested quickly. 'I'm a hot, sweaty mess!'

'Nope, you look beautiful. Very authentic.' Bridie took aim again. 'They'll be perfect for your website bio. I'm a website whizz if you need any help setting one up.'

It was on her list of things to do. Later. 'I need to do a good job first, otherwise the best landscape-design website in the world isn't going to help build my business.'

'I'll mock one up. I'd be happy to. Photos speak.'

Bridie Starr's landscape originals sold for thousands. 'I know what your pictures are worth. I can't afford you,' Ari stated bluntly.

Bridie pointed the camera right at Ari and the camera took a dozen or so shots in rapid succession. 'I'm doing it for free.'

'Why? I don't even *know* you.'

'Yeah, but I know Reid. He's one of my favourite people. Which, by the way, I'm so glad I get to speak with you in private, because I want you to keep an eye on him. He's been told to rest and take it easy. No bright sunshine in his eyes.'

'And you brought him *here*?'

'Sunglasses,' said Bridie, waving Ari's protest away. 'He even has goggles; provided you can get him to wear them in public. Not too much physical exertion for him either. And maybe some of these outdoor areas could be developed with shade cloth and roofing. Deep, deep shade and sensory stuff. Scents and textures and the like.'

'You mean a garden for the blind?' That definitely hadn't been in the brief. 'Just how bad *is* his eyesight?'

'Reid's guarding that knowledge pretty closely. He's so good at adapting that it's hard to catch him out, but I think it's worse than he's letting on.' Bridie offered a quick smile. 'Most of all I wanted to warn you that he's grouchy, frustrated with the slowness of his recovery, and don't be surprised if he disappears into the darkest bedroom every now and then because his head or his leg or his arm is killing him. Not that he'd ever dream of mentioning it. He's Outback tough.'

'Uh-huh.'

'Judah's the same—weakness must never be shown.'

'Uh-huh.'

'And here comes my darling man now.' Bridie looked to the sky. 'He's early.'

'How long is Reid planning to stay? You said something about being here overnight?'

'That was his original plan. A quick trip to see how you were getting on, little bit of fresh-food delivery, a little bit of flirting if I know Reid, although Gert's given him strict instructions to behave. It'd be great if you could keep him for a week. A week of rest would do him the world of good.'

'You want me to keep a grumpy billionaire occupied here for a *week* when he thought he was staying a *day*?' The woman had way too much faith in Ari's powers of persuasion.

Bridie's smile turned into a beatific grin. 'Everyone needs a challenge. And I can't wait to see the new landscaping you come up with. It's going to be brilliant.'

'You don't know that,' Ari protested as Bridie turned and headed back the way they'd come. 'This is the first real landscape I've ever been let loose on.'

'Yeah, but I have the best feeling about you. You've got this, Ari. I'm a believer.'

Reid watched the helicopter rise with a sharp pang of envy as Bridie and Judah flew away. He'd taken the freedom of being a pilot with an endless supply of aircraft at his disposal for granted and now he was grounded. Couldn't even drive a farm ute, according to Bridie, never mind that he'd had this particular work truck kitted out with the latest self-driving features. He'd been all for testing its off-road capacity this morning on a solo run to visit Ari, but once Bridie had got wind of his intentions she'd invited herself along for the ride.

She'd come in handy, though, he had to admit. Getting bogged in loose sand twice within the first five kilometres of the trip hadn't been encouraging.

The self-driving system hadn't been able to navigate a vaguely visible track through loose dirt and sand with any degree of clarity.

Bridie had insisted on driving them after that

second off-road adventure, while Reid had to sit there and mime being okay with not being able to contribute in any meaningful way. He'd been so very patient when it came to his rate of healing, but as improvement slowed his confidence had started to erode.

With Ari, in particular, he wanted to stand before her as a vibrant, physically robust man who could see every little bit of the world around him. How could he read her emotions when he could barely recognise a smile at twenty paces? If he wanted to read the expression in her eyes, he had to get within kissing distance, and what if she didn't want him to smash through her personal-space boundaries?

But if he didn't get close enough to see her expression, how could he know whether Ari was glad to see him?

She'd kept contact with him to a minimum during the time she'd been out here.

Was she simply a doggedly independent soul or actively avoiding him?

She was treating him like the client he was, with a progress report at the end of her first week, but he wanted to be so much more.

Just knowing she was out here made him want to be here too. Sure as hell, *that* had never happened to him before, although he'd seen it before in Judah when it came to wanting to be where Bridie was.

Reid wasn't quite ready to admit to being head over heels for Ari, but he couldn't stop thinking about her.

She'd had to get the plant cuttings she'd taken from channel country earlier that day out of her ute, she'd said awkwardly once Bridie had left. Did she need to plant them as well? Put their stems in water? He hadn't asked. He'd been too busy trying to ignore the spiking pain behind his eyes.

An hour later she still hadn't returned and his vision was shot and his leg ached so much that he was seriously reconsidering his flat-out refusal to use a walking aid, and... *Dammit, why was he so weak?*

A knock sounded on the screen door between kitchen and deck. 'Can I come in?' Ari asked.

'Of course.'

She'd changed her clothes and now wore a yellow T-shirt and a plum-coloured skirt instead of khaki work trousers and shirt. She'd pulled her hair back into a ponytail and wore a colourful chunky bracelet on her slender wrist.

The fact that she'd changed clothes and added jewellery had to mean she was glad to see him, surely?

'Come in.' She hadn't found him flat on his

back, and his ego liked that. Granted, he was only filling the ceramic water dispenser that sat next to the sink. The tap hose was one of those stretchy ones, so it wasn't exactly difficult. All he'd had to do was remove the lid, point and shoot.

'They're good, aren't they? Those water-filter set-ups,' she said as she entered the room.

'You want a glass?'

'No, I'm good.' She came closer, resting her pert behind against the side of the counter on his other side. 'You didn't tell me you were coming. I'd have baked a cake.'

'Are you pleased to see me?' If he couldn't rely on his sight for information, he'd have to get it some other way.

'I am *extremely* pleased to see you. But I do have a confession to make.'

'Tell me.'

She smiled in his direction. 'I hurt my shoulder this morning, trying to pull out a—um, probably not a great idea to tell you I don't know the name of the plant. The point is it took a lot of pulling and I have a sore shoulder.'

He wasn't sure where this conversation was going but he tried to pre-empt her, nonetheless. 'You want a massage?'

'No, the hot shower did a world of good but now I want to lie down on a bed and move my arm around and find my shoulder's happy place. I used to dislocate it all the time as a kid.'

'You have a dislocated shoulder?'

'No, but it's about to pop, I can feel it, and I'd rather it didn't. You could lie next to me while I see to it. We could hold hands, just like old times. And if need be, you can grab my arm above the elbow and pull.'

It sure as hell sounded like a dislocated shoulder, but he was up for it. 'Whatever you need.'

They ended up side by side on their backs on the bed, with the window shutters closed to the heat of the day, and at last he could close his eyes and drop the pretence of being able to function normally. He could feel her moving her arm about but she didn't encroach on his space, and he didn't reach for her hand.

He wasn't needy.

Not like before.

He didn't want Ari to think him weak.

But her hand—presumably the one attached to her good arm—reached for his and chivalry demanded he reciprocate. That was what he told himself as simple contentment invaded his body. For all the many ideas and projects that had consumed him over the years, all his restless travelling, he'd never felt so at peace as he did with Ari's hand wrapped in his. 'How's your shoulder?' he murmured. 'Do I need to pull?'

'I think it's okay. How's your headache?'

He made a feeble attempt to muster his defences, but he was too far down the contentment hole to rally more than a mental shrug. 'How did you know?'

'It's written on your face.'

'Bridie didn't notice.'

'You keep telling yourself that, precious. She's lovely, and she cares about you, and believe me she noticed. She asked me to persuade you to stay a week.'

'What did you say?'

'Told her she was dreaming if she thought I could get you to do anything you didn't want to do. But I'm not against the idea of you being here for a while. I'll still have to work—my client deserves something extraordinary and I'm determined to give it to him, and I'll probably put you to work on that too, but my evenings are free. Afternoons too, if I make an early start. Of course, there's no lap pool or health-spa facilities, but I have thoughts on turning an old water trough into an outdoor bath, so there's that. I think an outdoor shower after a hard day's work would be another welcome water addition. It's dusty out there.'

'Exactly how soon do you expect this outdoor bathing area to appear?'

'Well, my client needs to approve the concept

and after that it depends how much money he's got to throw at the proposal, y'know? There are budget versions that any stockman from around here would appreciate.'

'And the water? Where's that coming from?'

'The boss's last landscape designer put a gorgeous greywater filtering system in place but didn't understand the soil out here. I can make it work. Am I putting you to sleep?'

Maybe she *could* read his face after all. 'Almost.'

'Sleep. I'll be around when you wake up.'

'Last time I did that I ended up in a hospital bed two thousand kilometres away. *Without you.*'

'Well, you will choose the best surgeons.'

She made him laugh and his head ached because of it. 'How's your shoulder?'

'You're going to have to sit up, put one of your feet in my armpit, and pull on my arm.'

'Let's do it.' Before he lost the will to move. He got into position—he'd done this before—and within moments it was done with barely a whimper on his part.

Ari didn't whimper at all, just sighed when he eased back down beside her and took her hand.

'Have you taken pain tablets yet?' she asked.

'Half an hour ago.'

'Do you need more?'

'Can't.' He was under strict directions to take

them *only as directed*. Maybe he *had* been pushing his body a little too hard in an attempt to camouflage weakness. Maybe now was a good time to stop.

'I'll get you a cold pack from my cabin.'

'Are you trying to heal me again, with whatever you have lying around?'

'Hey, whatever works.' He could feel her getting up but he didn't open his eyes. 'Back in five.'

'Five minutes, you say?'

She squeezed his hand. 'I promise.'

CHAPTER ELEVEN

REID WAS FAST asleep when Ari returned. She put the cold pack and a glass of water on his bedside table and left him to his healing.

Returning to work, Ari picked up where she'd left off, planting cuttings into circular hollows in the ground, lined with fallen leaves and a thin layer of clay soil she'd found a few hundred kilometres east. Busy work, but she'd never felt more confident about her choice of career and the possibilities in front of her.

Reid was here, and while this was very much his world, it was hers too.

He found her as the sun hit the horizon, sending hot streaks across the sky. He took a long look at her plant nursery pits, and then looked at her and said, 'Okay, I'm a believer in the outdoor bathing idea. You're covered in mud.'

'Knew you'd see it my way. Your scientist and researchers also come back covered in mud at the end of the day. I've been stumbling upon them and doing informal surveys. If there was an out-side shower area, they'd use it.'

'Tell me more during dinner.'

He then coaxed her to dine with him once she was presentable by promising baked fish, fresh salad, and mangoes for dessert.

She showered quickly and made her way to the lodge he'd claimed for his stay. There were only two lodges at this site, with the other one remaining empty until his arrival.

'Iced tea or something stronger?' he asked as she entered his kitchen. 'I'm sticking to water.'

'Because of your medication?'

'That and a heartfelt desire to avoid another head-cracker.'

Made sense. He'd lost the tension in his body and his eyes had lost their haze of pain. She watched him plate up the baked fish with a surety born of long practice. 'How's the sister search?' she asked, when he set the meals on the table and held out a chair for her.

'Full of dead ends. Judah's taken the lead on it,' he admitted as he took a seat and waited for her to start eating before picking up his cut-lery. Pretty manners that she didn't fully under-stand—they served mainly to emphasise Reid's social class and her lack of any.

And then she remembered the story about him taking his brother to the roadside diner and nervously ordering everything on the menu. And how she'd been with him when he'd wolfed down Thai starters and terrible passionfruit beer at the swimwear store. He was the same man.

And this time the food was great, and she wanted his company and so what if she didn't quite know where the fishbones would be found? It was barramundi. Wasn't as if the fish bones were going to be small.

Ari favoured eating over talking—probably another no-no in polite society, but it had been a big day and she was hungry. Only once she'd cut grooves into the juicy flesh of mango cheeks and flipped the skin and devoured her half—and Reid's half too, when he declined his—did idle chat turn serious.

'So, no progress on the sister hunt but I did discover something interesting about the money my father gave your mother just after you were born. Could be nothing. Could be something. Want to hear it?' he asked.

Ari paused, sweet mango juice dripping down her chin as she put the fruit back on her plate and attempted to clean her sticky face and fingers with a napkin the size of a tissue. Reid wordlessly handed his napkin to her and waited for her answer.

She'd loved her mother dearly—but there was no pretending that her mother's life choices had always played out in Ari's favour. The stepfamily situation was a classic example of that. 'I don't know if I want to hear it. Is it going to shatter all my illusions?'

'Maybe.'

Again, he waited for her response. 'I guess I could stand to know more.'

'We have a forensic accountant looking through old financial records,' he told her. 'The money my father gave your mother came from a bank account owned by an Australian business called FNQ metals. My father held that money in his account for just under twenty-four hours before passing it through to your mother. At first, I thought it was a one-off transaction—a gambling debt paid in full, say—and my father had simply flipped it to your mother as thanks for not letting him gamble his home away. But there were other deposits from that account over the years, smaller amounts, same day each year, and they were all passed through to your mother within twenty-four hours. Is there anything special about the twenty-fourth of May?'

'It's my birthday.'

'Ah.' He seemed pleased. 'Figured it might be.'

'Meaning…what, exactly?'

'I think someone used my father to deliver money to your mother on your birthday. Still want to hear more?'

She took a quick sip of her iced tea, for courage. 'Is there more?'

'FNQ Metals is a publicly traded company these days but before that it belonged to a guy called Deacon Murray. He started out as a travelling stock contractor through Far North Queensland and the Northern Territory. He married at nineteen and he's still married to that same woman. He has three sons, now in their thirties. He made enough money out of cattle to buy himself a mining lease. It coughed up not just iron ore but copper and zinc as well. This is all public knowledge. My father had no business dealings with him at all beyond the money that went to your mother.'

She knew where this was going. 'You think this Murray guy is my father?'

How much of her could Reid actually see when he looked at her so steadily? Could he see her panic? All the hope and pain and years of wondering? Trying to discover clues in her dead mother's belongings?

'I think you should go online and look at some of the pictures of Deacon Murray and his kids. Then, if you want me to put an investigator on his whereabouts around the time your mother got pregnant, I will.'

This day was just full of surprises.

She traced her finger down the side of her

glass and studied Reid from beneath her lashes. She needed a bit of a shield while his information sank in. 'Do I look like him?'

'A bit. You look like one of his boys more.' Reid sat back. 'I think he took his mining business public so he could get the money to set you and your mother up. I suspect he did it through my father because your mother refused his direct offer of financial assistance.'

She took a deep breath. 'That's a lot of wondering.'

'Like I said, I can put someone on it and get you some facts. You could be a rich man's daughter.'

She'd always wanted to know who her father was. She'd never imagined him rich or successful. In her eyes he'd always been a handsome no-good drifter who'd known nothing about siring a daughter.

If Reid's speculations were true, then Deacon Murray had known all about Ari and hadn't come anywhere near her. 'You're absolutely brutal when it comes to making me question my identity.'

'Is that a bad thing?'

She pushed away from the table and headed for the deck. She wanted the cover of darkness as she worked through her emotions. Reid joined her, wary and watchful.

'Talk to me,' he said as he leaned against the railing.

'He knew about me. He's never been near me.' That was the most devastating revelation. 'And maybe he tried to help financially, and it did a bit and got spread around between others too. All to the greater good, right? But I'm an adult now and he owes me nothing, and your father's been dead for years and surely money can't still be coming in. I don't know what to do with this information.' She leaned against the railing of the deck and looked to the stars in the sky. There were millions of them in an Outback sky. On most nights a person could see them very clearly.

But Reid wasn't looking at the stars. When she glanced his way, he was looking at her. 'You could reach out to him.'

'And say what? All that money you sent amounted to *nothing*? He's not going to want me.'

'I wouldn't say that.'

But Ari was past listening. 'He made his choice when I was born. *Money's not care.* It's just a convenient way to paper over guilt.'

Reid blew out a breath. 'I thought you'd be pleased.'

'Well, I'm not! Your family history probably goes back hundreds of years. You know who you are. Everything's legit. You don't understand what it's like to not know who your father is and dream about some day connecting with him. In the good dreams my father is thrilled to discover he has a daughter. He's a wonderful man and he's thrilled to meet me.' She choked back a bitter laugh.

'What happens in the bad dreams?'

'In the bad dreams he's known about me from the beginning, and he just doesn't care.' She couldn't stand to let Reid watch her fall apart. 'Thanks for the meal. I have to go now.'

'Ari, wait. Let me—'

'You can't fix this!' He didn't deserve her anger. 'I'm sorry. I have to go.'

'When you say go, do you mean get in your ute and drive away?' he asked carefully.

'No.' She waved a hand in the direction of her cabin. It was too dark to drive without getting lost. She wasn't insane. 'I'm just going to my— your—' Aw, screw it. 'I just want to fall apart somewhere you can't see me, okay? I'm going to my room.'

'Okay.'

Okay.

She'd made her way to the steps when he spoke again. 'Ari, the money's not nothing. Murray wasn't so wealthy back then that he could fling it around without a care.'

She bit her tongue in an effort to keep harsh,

hurtful words like *You would know* from tumbling out.

Don't shoot the messenger. Don't lash out with words you don't mean. Stick to the ones you do mean.

'I'm sorry you get to see this side of me. I'm bitter and ungrateful and I don't give a damn about any money he might have sent. Money on my birthday? Why didn't my mother *tell me*? She didn't want me to know anything about him and he didn't want me at all.' So much for retreating to her room before hot tears threatened to spill. 'That's just betrayal.'

'Feelings are messy and very, very real,' he countered quietly. 'For some people, myself included, it's always tempting to run off and try to deal with them alone.' He favoured her with a crooked smile. 'You should talk to Bridie about hiding in your room. She hid in her room for years.'

Teenager Bridie Starr had been the beautiful, traumatised shut-in, forcing herself to step outside so she could take photos to send to the imprisoned man who'd saved her life—Ari knew the story. 'I'm not going to hide in my room for years because my father never claimed me.' It was probably too late to hide her emotions from the man in front of her, too.

'I'd like to walk you to your room,' he said gently. 'If I may.'

'Bad idea.'

'Is it?'

'I'd probably drag you inside and shamelessly demand that you help me forget all my lineage and make me feel wanted.'

His eyes gleamed. 'Oh, *really*?'

That was a yes from him. Ari suddenly felt very short of breath and it wasn't because she was about to start weeping.

'Happy to help,' he offered gravely. 'In fact, as a gentleman, I *insist*.'

Hell, yes. And she was going to take him up on his offer. To hell with muddying the waters between contractor and client. She wanted this. No, she needed this.

Ari *deserved* this.

He'd only wanted to help. All the digging he'd done, all the tracking down of information that he hadn't outsourced to anyone else... In all sincerity, Reid had imagined he was helping Ari. It had never once occurred to him that this new knowledge would hurt her.

All he wanted to do now was fix her.

They walked to her bedroom in silence, and once there Reid drew her into his arms and sought her lips with his. It started off as apology and comfort, but all it took was Ari's passionately uninhibited response for it to spiral out of his control and become something else entirely.

Gentle caresses became greedy ones as he slid his hands beneath her clothes and honoured the warmth of her skin and the shape of her body. So smooth and warm, utterly responsive as he set his lips to the underside of her jaw and traced his way to her collarbone. Her scent a tease, the way she melted against him an aphrodisiac.

He'd never been so invested in a woman's pleasure as he picked her up and she wound her legs around him. He tumbled them onto the bed and began shedding clothes, and so did she, and that first full slide of skin against skin was almost Reid's undoing.

Women liked him and he liked them. He'd made a point of knowing how to please them. But none had ever wielded the power over him that Ari did. Undoing him so completely that he struggled to think, let alone plan ahead.

He would taste every inch of her—was that a thought worth following? It worked for a while, until he reached her breasts and discovered that the edge of his tongue could make her wild with need. He let her roll him on his back as he closed his lips around her and suckled, and moments later soft warmth covered his hardness as she rocked against him seeking friction.

That plan worked brilliantly for both of them—maybe from now on he would let Ari make all the plans all the time when it came to bedroom contact. That fleeting thought lasted the time it took for her to line him up so he could slide into her tight heat, an action that ripped a groan from the depths of his soul as he rolled with her until she lay beneath him and let purest instinct take over.

When Ari crested, he was moments behind her, and it wasn't his finest, most considered performance, but it was hands down the most intense sexual experience of his life. His brain was fried, his body exhausted, and he couldn't stop smiling.

It was his first, fumbling experience with sex all over again—dialled up to a hundred.

'That was—' no way was he about to admit he might have been doing sex all wrong…until now '—illuminating.'

'I'll say.'

Was she smiling? He turned his head and when he couldn't quite tell, he reached out and traced her lips with questing fingers. 'Stop it,' he murmured when she nibbled them. 'I'm trying to tell if you're satisfied. Are you smiling?'

She flowed into his arms and tucked her head

beneath his chin and placed her hand over his heart. 'With all my heart.'

'Because you're satisfied?'

'Because you make me happy.'

'Because I want to be sure you're satisfied. If you're not, I could do other things to you until my poor, broken body is ready for more.'

'Oh, well, then.' This time he could *feel* her smile against his chest. 'I could probably be *more* satisfied. I wouldn't want you to have any doubts.'

'You're sure?' He ran his fingers over her body until he reached her knee and then he scooted down and let her leg below her knee drape over his shoulder as he pressed a teasing kiss against her inner thigh.

'Do what you have to do.' Her words ended on a gasp.

He flicked her centre with his tongue and felt her arch against his hands so he did it again, exposing her with his thumb to better access his target. 'You're sure you're sure?' Her hands clutched at the bedsheet beneath them as he blew against the sensitive, swollen flesh.

'I'm sure!'

And still he hesitated, because teasing her was just too satisfying. For him.

'Would you like me to beg?' she demanded,

and now there was a thought he could get behind in full.

'Yes.' Satisfaction laced his voice at the wonder that was Ari Cohen in his bed. 'I certainly would.'

Reid stayed on for five more sex-soaked days. He spent his spare time dictating extra parameters to the self-drive programming so that his ute didn't drive off into a sand bank every five minutes. Ari spent her days working on a landscape plan, eventually abandoning her idea of presenting him with computer drawings in favour of explaining what she wanted to do with various areas as they walked through them—once in the morning, once at noon, and then again at night. He approved the plans with all his heart, rejected any suggestion of her doing the hard labour required, and together they put together a team of former stockmen, fencers, and tradesmen willing to spend two weeks on the job and get it done.

They butted heads on whether Ari should stay on or turn both lodges over to the team of workers.

Ari argued there was absolutely no reason for her to leave and every reason in the world to supervise. Reid claimed she should take Gert's old room at his homestead and let the guys have their privacy, and *sure* it would mean a four-hour round trip every day but those were the breaks.

He knew he was being ridiculous as they fought about trust, and security, and stereotypes. He didn't know how to swallow his concerns until Ari picked up the phone and called her former lab partner, Sarah, who might well be looking for a bit of work or know of someone who was. Half an hour later, Ari had two more female labourers in place and Sarah's sister, who was a plumber with her own earthmoving equipment, had been signed up to the job too.

Reid tripled the labour costs on the contract Ari had prepared, signed it, and the arguing stopped, and the lovemaking resumed.

Reid was utterly, irrevocably putty in the hands of Ari Cohen.

If it hadn't been for a raft of medical appointments with specialists far busier than him, he'd have stayed on.

Instead, he arranged for Ari to come to Brisbane at the end of the following week to view the copper birdbath she wanted to install, never mind that she'd already ordered it.

'You just want to see me again,' she teased, but he had absolutely no defence against her words.

It was nothing but the truth.

CHAPTER TWELVE

'Hmm.'

Reid hated the *hmm*s of eye specialist Fink with a vengeance.

It wasn't that the man was a bad conversationalist; the doc could string long sets of words together when he wanted to. And given that Fink was the best eye specialist the country had to offer, Reid trusted that the man knew what he was talking about, even if Reid sometimes needed a dictionary.

Had Reid thought his eyesight was improving, those *hmm*s during this latest examination would have registered as confirmation that all was coming along as expected. They might have been tolerable.

But Reid's vision had not been improving, his headaches were becoming more frequent, and no amount of 'positive thinking' and 'mindful recovery' was going to wish those undeniable facts out of existence.

Reid kept his chin on the rest pad and stared at the bright light he'd been told to stare at as the slit lamp machine clicked and whirred and took pictures of the inside of his eyeballs.

'Okay, we're done.'

When the doctor rolled away, still in his chair, and turned towards a wall-mounted computer screen, Reid came to stand alongside him. Not that Reid had much chance of seeing what the older man saw unless he stood a whole lot closer, but if it helped Fink make his diagnosis and explain what was happening, Reid was all for staring at the screen right along with him.

'I haven't made any headway at all with my eyesight this month, have I?' asked Reid as the doctor studied the screen and said nothing.

'Correct.'

Not the best news he'd ever heard. 'Why not?'

Fink turned to look at him. 'Best guess? Your original head trauma and cranial nerve damage was too severe for you to ever fully recover. You've made remarkable strides, Mr Blake, but the body's repair system has its limits. Your vision in your right eye is always going to be better than your left. The tunnel vision you now experience may not improve. Wear your eye patch again, doesn't matter which eye, and see if your headaches subside. Wear wraparound sunglasses day and night and note whether that too helps with the headaches.'

'I guess getting my driver's licence back is out of the question?' Initially, he'd believed he'd get there eventually but any last hope of that happening had been quietly fading.

'Son, I know what you want to hear. And I know some fool mental-health expert likely dangled that possibility in front of your nose like a carrot, but I'm going to go out on a limb here and stake my professional reputation on the notion that no one with any sense is ever going to let you control a vehicle again.'

'Noted.'

Hated.

'Would you like a second opinion on that?'

'No.' They were his eyes, after all. He was intimately acquainted with what they could and couldn't do. 'Did I tell you I've found the prettiest girl in the world?'

'Have you now? Well, it sounds like those eyes of yours may be good for something after all.' There was a smile in Fink's voice. 'I don't see any neurological evidence of deterioration, so don't be too disheartened by these latest results. No improvement may mean that your eyesight is stabilising and this is your new normal. Your eyesight test results may go back and forth a bit from now on, depending on the day and how tired you are. Do you have a headache now?'

'Yes.'

'Pain scale?'

'Five.'

'Have you taken any medication for it?'

'Not yet. Didn't want to juice my test results.'

'Stick to inventing engines, Mr Blake, and get the nurse to give you some ibuprofen on your way out.'

'Nah, I'm good. I'll take some when I get home.'

The doctor sighed. 'I know you Outback types have a built tough reputation to uphold, but do yourself a favour and next time you get a migraine take the medication I'm prescribing you.'

'Thanks, Doc, but I still have the last prescription you gave me. How about I just get that one filled?'

'Hmm,' said the good doc. 'Do.'

R and R. Rest and recovery. The only people who thought that was a positive thing hadn't endured endless months of being told to throttle down, kick back and relax, and hand control over to others.

Even Reid's Brisbane apartment that had been especially set up for rest and relaxation couldn't soothe him this morning.

Reid had found it especially hard to hand over the reins of the engineering company he'd built, never mind that the 'others' in question were reliable, visionary, and didn't *need* him at the helm. Reid had chosen his executives a little too well, and even people-shy Judah had stepped up to shoulder some of Reid's workload. This morning while eye doctor Fink had been telling Reid to take his pills like a good boy, Judah had been presenting the quarterly forecast to Reid's board of directors. Judah, whose knowledge of solar engines was sketchy at best, but who believed unconditionally in Reid's timeline for bringing those developments to the market.

Judah's strategy had been alarmingly simple. 'I go in, I tell them this is what you want, and they approve it. Easy.' Oh, to have been a fly on the wall at that meeting.

Judah meant well. He was working his arse off keeping all the Blake family enterprises running smoothly while Reid *recovered*. Stock prices were up, milestones were being met.

Business was booming along without him, and he shouldn't feel resentful about that, he just shouldn't. It was a measure of how good he was at building strong business foundations that they stood strong without him.

And yet…the longer his recovery, the more sidelined and useless he felt. Reid's confidence, his place in his family, was based on his ability to be the wunderkind. The kid who held it together. The young man with vision and work ethic. The mechanical genius who'd built a billion-dollar company using the contacts and start-up money his family had afforded him. He didn't want to be put out to pasture like a lame race-horse. He wanted to be part of something bigger than himself.

He needed to be sure of his worth.

And for the first time since he was seventeen years old and sitting across from his brother in a petrol-station diner, he questioned it.

Even Ari had taken the reins of her fledgling business and *shone*. She and her crew were busy creating an outdoor utopia on their sixth and final set of lodges. After that, Ari had another few weeks of rotating around the work sites as she made sure her gardens were growing as they should, and then she'd be gone. Her work was getting noticed, what with Bridie featuring it in her social-media stream, and magazines always keen for editorial featuring what was happening within the mystical Outback Blake empire.

A leg-up had well and truly been given, and Ari was now perfectly positioned to succeed.

Which left Reid's fairy godmother gig superfluous to requirements, and his Prince Charming feathers charred because he didn't waltz that well any more.

He'd tolerated being a wounded prince as best he could.

He actively hated the thought of being a permanently broken one.

He leaned against the kitchen counter of his Brisbane home and watched as Judah slung his tailored jacket over the back of a chair and headed for the fridge. Judah could still stare at a dinner menu for a long time before making his selection, but he had the contents of Reid's drinks fridge well and truly sorted. Kiwi and leafy greens go-go juice if he wasn't drinking alcohol, Crown Lager if he was. Apparently, it was a green juice kind of day.

'You have the board's backing, and the shareholders voted their approval,' Judah told him, and all Reid could do was nod listlessly, because this latest achievement didn't really have anything to do with him. 'Are you listening?'

'Yeah, of course. Good.'

But Judah wasn't having a bar of Reid's fake enthusiasm. 'I thought you'd be pleased.'

'I am. Hey, you want to go rock climbing at Kangaroo Point this afternoon?' The cliffs were a local climbing spot with great views of the city. 'We should celebrate the good news.'

Judah halted in the process of ditching his tie

and unbuttoning the top few buttons on his pristine business shirt. 'You're climbing again?'

'Yeah.' Reid tried to inject a little confidence into his reply. This would be his first attempt, but Judah didn't need to know that.

'Are you cleared to do that? What did the eye doctor say?'

'Yeah, he's really pleased with my progress. Everything's on the up.'

Judah shot him a sharp glance. 'And the headaches?'

'All part of the process.' Not lies, exactly. More like spin. He'd been cleared for moderate exercise. They sent beginners up Kangaroo Point all the time, no former climbing experience required—and Reid's climbing skills were well beyond that. His leg was getting stronger all the time and his dislocated shoulder had been an easy fix. As for his eyes…tunnel vision could only help him focus on the cliff face in front of his nose. Reid wanted this challenge. He needed it.

'Who are you climbing with?'

'Jules.' Professional climbing instructor and indoor-climbing champion. 'She won't mind if you turn up.' Reid paid her enough not to mind, and Judah had climbed before, even if he hadn't taken to it the way Reid had.

Judah made a face. 'I can fit a climb in tomorrow morning. I still have a meeting with the EPA to get through this afternoon.'

'No drama. You do you, I'll do me.' Reid wasn't about to admit that Judah's presence had been a bright spot in a week full of medical appointments and increasingly bleak health news.

Reid needed a win. One tiny boost to help him feel functional again and *worth* something. 'It'll be fine.'

Ari didn't know if Reid had somehow set a satellite to hover over her location. She didn't know if satellites could do that, but not once in the past two months had Ari or any of her team lost phone or Internet connection.

Her team. She'd put together a core group of people who wanted to keep working for her and her next project was to landscape a visitors' centre for a small town with a big grant geared towards it becoming a tourist gateway to channel country. After that, she'd locked in a job on Queensland's Sunshine Coast for a local celebrity. Five acres of hinterland scrub to tame and Ari was there for it. And maybe it was the generous pay or the travel or the way people had clicked, but her trade crew were there for it too.

End of day meant getting online and checking out the weather report and whatever was trending by way of news. Ari usually did it while throwing together something to eat, but today her appetite was skewered by the headline on her phone.

'Billionaire Tycoon Takes Another Fall.'

There were two photos to go with the headline—one was of a group of people gathered at the top of a cliff. The other picture was an old headshot of Reid in a tux.

He'd fallen off a cliff? No, a climbing accident. No. According to a spectator there'd been no dramatic fall. He'd been nearing the top of the climb and had seemed to pass out. His climbing partner and others had been on hand to help and eventually he'd finished the climb and been bundled into a waiting ambulance.

According to the reporter, he was in a stable condition.

The rest of the article was fairy floss about his numerous accomplishments, his ex-con billionaire brother, and his sister-in-law the world-class photographer.

Ari's hands shook as she dialled the number Reid had given her, but her call went to an answering machine and she didn't leave a message. She phoned Bridie next, and when the other woman answered, Ari could barely find the words.

'Hi.' Her voice shook, she sounded rough. 'It's Ari. I—' She didn't have any right to query. 'I saw the news.'

'You want to know about Reid?'

'Yes, please.'

'We're at the Princess Alexandria hospital. He's undergoing tests. He seems fine. He's beyond cranky—at the world and everyone in it—but fine.'

'What happened?'

'Hey, feel free to try and get medical information out of a grown man who doesn't want to talk about it. No, go ahead. I dare you.' Bridie sounded at the end of her wits.

'That bad?'

'Judah's on a tear because he's worried out of his mind. Reid's telling us to go away because he's *fine* but he can't sign his name on a hospital form because as far as I can tell he can barely see the lines.'

'I—' Would he want her there? With all that was going on? He'd never talked much about his injuries or his recovery. Beyond that first evening at the lodge when she'd lain down with him and he'd slept for a couple of hours, he'd acted as if he had no medical issues at all beyond some fuzzy or tunnel vision every now and again—he never had come clean on what he could and couldn't see. He'd never admitted to another headache. 'Can you tell him I called?'

'You want him to call you back?'

'Yes!' Too eager by far. 'I mean…'

'You mean yes,' Bridie said dryly. 'I'll let him know.'

'Thank you, I—' She wanted to be there so badly, but didn't know if she had the right. 'I'd like to come and see him.' The way she hadn't last time. Their relationship was new but surely she had the right to reach out by phone. Cheer him up in person if that was what he wanted from her. 'I'm worried about him.'

You're in love with him.

That too. All it had taken was the thought of never seeing him again to make that inescapably clear to her. 'Is it wrong to want to yell at him a bit?'

'By all means, *do*. We're all just tippy-toeing around being stoic and supportive and it's not working. I'm no doctor, but if you want my opinion he took on more than he could chew and doesn't want to admit it because he's embarrassed, and, Ari, I'm trusting you with this information because I know you'd never use it against him or take it to the press—'

'I would never.'

'I know.' Bridie sounded so *kind*. 'Reid's struggling to accept that he'll never be as fit and healthy and active as he was before. You're welcome to try to talk some sense in him but that might just put you in the firing line.'

'I'm used to being in the firing line. My stepfather was a mean drunk and he wasn't especially fond of me. Not that I want to bore you with baggage, or that I think Reid's anything like that. He's not,' Ari added hastily. 'But I can hold my own in an imperfect world. I'm not afraid of facing up to problems head-on. Unless it's about my birth father. Still picking at that big gaping wound, but I'm working on it. I'm tough and resilient and I get where I'm going eventually. I can start driving now. Be there in the morning.' Did any of that make sense? She didn't know.

'Anyway,' she continued quietly. 'I'll wait for his call.'

'He's having an MRI and I'll tell him you called. And when I get home I'll come find you and we'll catch up for a cuppa, okay?'

'Okay.' Ari had the sinking feeling that the only thing she'd accomplished with this phone call was to expose her crush on Reid for all to see. What if he wanted to keep their relationship a secret? What if it was just a fling—too new or too casual for Ari to be worming her way into his family unit and he didn't want to see her at all? 'Sure.'

He didn't ring back.

It took Ari another week to realise that Reid wasn't *going* to ring back.

The crew had finished their work on the last of

the eco-lodge locations and were packing up to return to Brisbane. Ari was in two minds about heading there too, but indecision had taken hold. What was she going to do? Knock on Reid's door and demand he let her in?

Yes.

He told you to trust him.

What if he's waiting for you to value him and be there for him the way he's been for you?

When her work crew headed east in raggedy convoy, Ari went with them.

Reid Blake wasn't expecting company, so when his security system pinged to let him know someone wanted in, he took his time getting out of the spa and grabbing a towel and heading for the security screen on the patio to see who it was. Bridie and Judah had finally headed home this morning after days of hanging around and making sure he had everything he needed to be going on with.

He saw doctors daily. He had a physio come and tend him twice a week.

Eye doctor Fink had seen him in the hospital and again at Reid's apartment two days ago. He'd toured Reid's loft workspace, asked questions about work and his daily routine, and then dictated a list of aids and devices for the sight impaired. He'd sent the audio file to Reid and told him to investigate new ways of getting on with it.

He'd asked Reid where the prettiest girl in the world was and *hmm*'d when Reid answered, 'Working. Doing her own thing, *like she should*.'

He didn't want Ari to see his weakness and his fear. He'd get around to seeing her again when he was good and ready, and that might be a good long while. Reid finished towelling off and leaned closer to the screen so he could see who was at the door.

And yet here she was.

Shorts and boots and T-shirt and backpack slung over one shoulder, dark sunglasses shading her eyes and her hair pulled back into a ponytail. She looked tired and dusty and strong and healthy and his heart just about split in two because he didn't want her here almost as much as he did want her here. And he didn't know what to do.

'Hey,' she said brightly when he opened the door. 'You've been swimming.'

His wet trunks were a dead giveaway, he supposed. 'Ari.' He pitched his reply just shy of cool. 'What brings you by?'

He didn't need to see the expression on her face to see the tensing of her shoulders or the straightening of her spine. 'I realise our relationship…friendship…whatever this is, was built on you turning up out of the blue unexpectedly. Do I not have leeway to do the same?' The words themselves weren't her only challenge. Her steady, forthright delivery called him on his less than enthusiastic greeting too.

Silently, he stood aside so she could enter. If he was truly going to go through with cutting her out of his life, better he didn't do it at the door with an audience potentially lurking nearby.

She headed for his kitchen, slinging her backpack on a stool before turning to face him, arms crossed in front of her and her feet planted wide as she surveyed him from head to toe and back again. 'You don't look like you're at death's door.'

'I'm not.'

'Good to know. You haven't been taking my calls. Not even my business ones.'

He hadn't been taking anyone's calls.

'Wallowing in a pit of self-pity and despair, Bridie called it.' She walked around him in a slow circle, as if studying a sculpture, and it was all he could do to stay still and relaxed. 'You can understand my concern, although I'd like to point out that your arse is still very fine, as is the rest of your appearance. Not that I'm shallow and attracted to you solely because of appearance, but I've seen you looking worse.'

'I'm fine.'

'I don't think so.'

'What do you want me to say?' he snapped. 'That my eyesight's shot?'

'Yes.' Her calmness was not rubbing off on him. 'Let's start there.'

Hot temper flashed in his eyes, and good. She was angry too, and if he couldn't see her well enough to see the signs, she'd simply have to provide him with verbal cues. 'You said you trusted me, and I believed you. You called me resourceful and resilient and worthy, and I believed that too. I needed a hand, and you gave it, unconditionally. We're friends and more.'

So much more and in such a short time. Maybe that was part of the problem.

She took a step closer. 'Why can't you trust me to be there for you?'

He took a careful step back. 'I don't want to argue with you.'

'I'm not arguing with you.' Even if she did sound fried. 'I'm arguing *for* you. For us, and a future we might share.'

And he couldn't let her win. 'I don't want to saddle anyone with having to stick by someone with my limitations. You're just starting out. Every good thing in this life is out there waiting for you.'

'But not you.'

'You'll be fine without me. Better than fine.'

'And here I thought I was going to be the reluctant one in this relationship,' she said. 'Never quite believing I was good enough. I've got no money. No connections. No unshakeable belief that I'm smarter or wiser or more talented than most other people. And yet somehow you made me believe that I can pull my weight and be valued and loved and wanted because I'm me. Ari. Why can't you be just you, battered and not seeing too well around the edges but whole—and lovable too?'

She was battering away at his defences as if they were matchsticks. He had to push her away before he crumbled in a pile at her feet, a pitiful, broken shell of a man who couldn't let a good woman go. 'You have a stepfather and step-brother who drove you from your home. A father you won't go near,' he snarled. 'You can't even fight your own demons. What chance would you have against mine?'

'Is that the argument you're going with? You're pushing me away because I'm not used to fighting for every scrap of love I've ever been gifted?' She stepped forward and poked a pointy finger into his chest. 'I can and will fight my own demons. You'll see. And then I'll be back for you. Maybe you can slay a couple of your own demons while I'm away.'

She headed for the door.

'You forgot your backpack.' But she didn't turn around. 'I built you a garden at site six. A sensory garden full of texture and shadows and water and sounds. It's a haven for relaxation and renewal, a place of majesty and tranquillity and I built it with all the love I have in my heart for you. The plans are in the backpack. Drawings, notebooks, pressed plants, jars of different coloured dirt that I used. Pictures of all the birds I've seen in the garden so far. Waterway plans and drainage. Pumps and pipes and everything else. So what if you can't see everything I've written? You're the one with endless resources. If you don't want to go and experience it for yourself, try getting someone to explain it to you.'

His doors didn't slam. They drew quietly closed with a good-mannered huff.

He leaned his back against it and pressed the heels of his hand against the sudden sting in his eyes.

She argued passionately, and for him, and he loved her for that. He loved her full stop. He'd figured that out at some point between the slaying of demons and the building of a tranquil garden just for him. But how could he keep her, and keep her happy, if he couldn't even see his own way forward?

He had to let her go. His shortcomings were not her responsibility.

She'd see that he was right.

Eventually.

CHAPTER THIRTEEN

ARI WAS HEARTBROKEN and Reid was a jerk, but she wasn't giving up. Sometimes growth came with reckonings and putting one step in front of the other and trudging through bad weather until blue sky broke overhead. Reid had his journey and she had hers, and as she drove west, out of the city, she reasoned that he had been right in some ways. She did still have personal problems of her own to tackle before demanding he tackle his. She was a successful, confident woman with a whole lot of love, energy and encouragement to give. She could do this.

Ari picked up her phone and put a call through to the one living person who'd never let her down. 'Hi, Gert, I was wondering if I can come and visit for a few days?'

'You know you can.' Gert's voice grounded her. 'When?'

'Tomorrow? I'm heading back from Brisbane. I'll stay in a motel overnight.'

'I thought you were still at Cooper's Crossing.'

'We finished up yesterday and lit out. It's all done. I wanted to give Reid the good news.'

'How is he?'

'Grouchy. Finding it hard to come to terms with what his accident has taken from him.' She might explain more when she got there. She wasn't sure how much Gert knew about Ari's relationship with Reid. Ari hadn't been hiding it—she'd simply been working hard and out of reach of the real world for most of it.

'Had to happen eventually,' Gert said with a sigh. 'That boy always did present his bright side to others, even after taking some mighty hard knocks. As if people wouldn't tolerate having him around if he wasn't all sunshine and light.'

She hadn't thought of it that way. Something else to chew on during the long drive home and take with her when next she saw him.

'I want to drop in on Patrick and Jake.' Her stepfather and stepbrother. 'Clear some air if I can. Put the whole lot behind me if I can't.'

'About that.' Gert paused as if choosing her words carefully. 'You might want to reconsider. Patrick's been on a bender for days.'

Ari closed her eyes. 'What set him off this time?'

'Who knows? He's not a good man.'

'He might have been once upon a—'

'No, Ari. That man drank the money set aside for your education, threw you out of the home your mother owned the minute she died, and threatened his son with a beating if they so much as acknowledged you.'

'Jake's been nodding at me when he sees me these days. He's almost eighteen. I can be there with a helping hand if he wants out.'

'He spat on you.'

'He was *ten*.' Ari had never expected her little stepbrother to defend her when Patrick had turned mean. Granted, she'd never expected her step-sibling to spit on her either, but if it had kept him in his father's good graces, she could understand the why of it. Neither her nor Jake had been driving the animosity. Someone else had been directing the roles they had to play.

'I want to help. I want to offer Jake a labouring job on my crew when we do the gardens at the visitors' centre.'

'That'd be like asking him to declare war on his father.'

'I know. And maybe he'll spit on me again, but I'm still going to offer him a way out of his father's grasp, same way you offered me one.'

There was a long, long pause. 'I'll back you,' said Gert finally. 'Let's fight for him.'

'Gert…' Her aunt waited for her to continue.

'Have you ever heard of a man named Deacon Murray?'

'Doesn't ring a bell.'

'Look him up on the web. See if his face is familiar.'

'Why?'

'I think he might be my biological father. I think I'm going to write to him. Ask him what happened and why he sent money—a lot of money—via Reid's father, but never came near me. See what happens.'

'Are you expecting anything from him?'

'Not a damn thing beyond answers—if that's who he is. I'm just...building the me I want to be, going forward. I owe it to myself to face my demons head-on, right? And clear the way to move forward with confidence in my own value. Enough self-esteem to let love in. Lead by example, even.'

That was what she wanted out of all of this.

'I'll see you when you get here,' said Gert. 'Drive carefully.'

Ari dialled the next number as she paced a three-star roadside motel room. It was clean enough for the faint smell of cheap disinfectant to tease her nostrils. Good enough for her even if she had spent the past few months living from one lovely architect-designed eco lodge to the next.

She didn't need access to luxury. Not from Reid, not from the father she'd never met. She wanted honesty instead.

She had no private number for Deacon Murray, but she did have a business number.

A female voice answered. Receptionist? Personal assistant? Wife? Who knew? 'Hi. My name is Ari Cohen and I'd like to speak with Mr Deacon Murray, if he's in.'

'Is he expecting your call, Ms Cohen?'

Ari could work with polite professionalism. 'I expect not, but if you could tell him I called, that would be great. Ari Cohen, from the Barcoo. I'd like to email my contact details through to you as well.'

'Not a problem, Ms Cohen. I can certainly let him know you called and get those details to him.'

Applause for the super-efficient woman, whoever she was.

Ari tossed her mobile on the threadbare bedspread and pushed her hair from her face. She wasn't finished facing her fears by any means. But it was a start.

It was ten past six in the afternoon and Ari still had a hundred kilometres of dirt road to drive before she reached Gert's when her mobile phone rang and an unfamiliar number lit up the screen.

She eased her foot off the accelerator and let the vehicle ease to a stop. No need to get off the road, not out here. No need to even stop, she decided, as she picked up and said hello. It could be a potential client, and, if so, she needed to be available to them. 'ARI Landscaping, Ari speaking.'

Nothing.

'Hello?' Her reception was iffy.

'Ari Cohen?' The man cleared his throat and Ari held the phone a little further from her ear as she brought the car to a halt. 'This is Deacon Murray returning your call.'

Oh. Now it was her turn to get tongue-tied. 'Right.'

'I believe I know why you called. I've been waiting for it for a long time, wondering what I'd say when the moment came.'

He was going to say no.

'The thing is, I have three sons.'

Who needed a daughter when they had three sons?

'And a loving wife who's stood by me for over forty years.'

He was definitely going to deny ever knowing her mother.

'And I love them all very much.'

Why would he confess to giving Ari's mother any money? He'd pretend it was all Lord Blake's

doing and that he knew nothing about it. She
could see it coming a mile.

Deny. Deny. Deny.

Well, *bring it on*.

'I'm listening, Mr Murray.' To hell with giving him an out.

'What is it you want?' he asked with quiet def-
erence and made her frown.

'I want to know who my father is. If that person is you, I'd like to meet you in person so I can
count that question answered once and for all.'

He'd never agree to her request.

He cleared his throat again.

Men were cowards.

Honourable cowards were the worst.

'On behalf of my entire extended family, and
myself, I'd like to invite you to an informal barbecue lunch this Sunday at my home.' Quiet
words that rang with sincerity. 'We'd all like to
meet you very much.'

Ari was still in shock when she walked into
Gert's kitchen two hours later. She'd said yes
and hung up, because her feelings were threat-
ening to strangle her into silence. She had two
days to get her act together before meeting them
all in person. The man had eight grandkids, for
goodness' sake. Three daughters-in-law. His wife

bred dachshunds and there were puppies on the ground, did she want one?

It was all just a little too soon and definitely too much but no way was she letting the opportunity slip away. Regardless of whether they truly were as loving and accepting as they sounded, Ari would be there for it.

She'd almost forgotten what other wheels she'd put in motion—it had been one hell of a day—but the young man in Gert's kitchen brought her back to reality with a start.

'Jake.' She sought the older woman's gaze. 'Gert. Sorry I'm late. I got held up.'

'Perfect timing,' Gert replied with a wave of her arm towards the oven. 'I'm about to dish up.'

Ari dropped her duffel beside the door and went to the bathroom to clean up, and when she returned, Jake was carving meat while Gert added serving spoons to salad greens and cheesy potato bake.

It wasn't until halfway through the meal, with Gert providing most of the conversation, that Ari stitched together the scattered remnants of her will and turned to her silent stepbrother, who'd eaten quickly, with his eyes lowered and his head down, giving clear signals to those who knew how to look for them that he had no idea where his next decent feed was coming from.

'I have a landscaping business now and a really good team of tradies who work with me.' Her goal was to put the offer to him, tell him why she was making it, and leave the rest up to him. 'I need a labourer for a job we have coming up at the visitor information centre at Black Ridge.'

'What's the pay?' He didn't look at her.

'The award wage for someone your age plus a living away from home allowance that all my employees get. I can send you the job description and the wage breakdown if you're interested.' She'd be calling the shots. 'It's pretty simple garden labour, but if you won't take orders from me and have no intention of working hard, don't take the job. You won't last a day. I'll make sure of it.' She refused to let him disrupt her crew with family angst.

She wondered whether or not to touch on their not so happy past. Probably best to open that wound wide and see if she could flush out the rot. 'You were only a kid when I left home. I don't know you very well and you don't know me. But I do know your father's faults and his fury and what he does to drive people away. I'm trusting Gert's judgment when she says you're not like him.'

His head came up, his brown eyes direct and his boyish jaw hard. He was well on his way to becoming a strong, handsome man who looked a lot like his father. 'I'm not like him.'

'Be sure.'

She saw fierce determination and hope in his eyes. 'I'm not like him,' he repeated. 'I'll work hard for you. I want the job.'

'You'll start next Tuesday, helping me source plants and order materials.'

The faintest of smiles crossed his lips. 'Looking forward to it.'

'Eat up,' said Gert, her expression warmly approving.

Maybe taming demons of old wasn't so difficult after all.

CHAPTER FOURTEEN

THE PROBLEM WITH arguing with Ari and watching the door close behind her was that Reid still had business ends to tie up and they still needed to deal with one another on a professional basis. Reid had promised her she wouldn't be disadvantaged should a romance between them go bad. So far, he hadn't lived up to his promise at all, but he would.

Soon.

For the first time in his life he'd allowed his sister-in-law to sweep into his life and scoop him up and take him home to Jeddah Creek station. Not that it was his home any more but as the family seat in Australia it held all the treasures and memories of his childhood home.

In retrospect, his Kangaroo Point climb had been a terrible idea, useful only for exposing his physical frailty for all to see. Business had suffered. He'd pushed friends away, craving solitude and room to heal outside the public gaze.

He'd even tried to push Judah and Bridie away, but they were having none of it.

He appreciated their efforts to make him feel essential to the family unit, but more than anything he'd wanted to lie on a bed with Ari and hold her hand and say *I don't know how to be who I used to be* out loud. He wanted to say *I need to create the new me but I'm tired for the first time in my life and there's a black dog licking at my heels.*

He wanted to turn her into a what? A nursemaid? A whipping post for every frustration? What kind of person would he be if he did that to someone he—?

Someone he loved.

Far better to lie around in dark rooms and pretend he was doing just what the doctor ordered. Resting. Relaxing.

Spiralling into the darkest depression.

His bedroom door opened but he made no move to open his eyes. Bridie wouldn't have entered without knocking first. Judah wasn't home. It could only be one other rather small person with no notion of the boundaries he was so desperate to enforce. 'Uncle Reid,' a little voice whispered. 'Are you awake?'

'Yes.' He tried to make a point of not lying to minors.

'Are you hiding?'

'No.' So much for telling the truth. 'What's up?'

'Have you seen Fluffy-Wuffy?'

The grey terror? Bane of his brother's life? Currently fast asleep on his back on Reid's bed, and using Reid's leg as a hot-water bottle? It was tempting, very tempting to say no. 'He's here.'

'He naps a lot.' Piper ventured closer. 'So do you.'

This was true. Maybe Reid could ease back into truth-telling after all. 'Yes. I'm resting and relaxing.'

'Mum says that just because you look better, doesn't mean you are.' She'd reached the bed, her hand reaching out to pat the cat, who started purring up a storm.

'She's right.' A pox on truth-tellers young and old.

'Can you see good any more?'

Had she heard Bridie discussing that or had her own observations led to the obvious conclusion? 'No. But I'm a rebel. One day I'll make a robot eye that can see for me.'

'I'm going to be a rebel too,' Piper declared, and Reid smiled at her confident declaration. He had no doubt that his niece would test boundaries all her life. Judah tried to hold a strong and sensible line, Bridie less so, but this child was already such a force to be reckoned with. As an heiress to billions, would she grow up to resent people seeing her as a bank teller machine, wanting to be around her as a pathway to wealth and status? Or would she weed them out, as Reid had done over the years?

Would she find the Aris of this world without having to land at their feet in a broken heap?

He hoped so.

'Do you want to play truck drivers with me?'

Did he have anything else to do?

Reid eased up onto one elbow, just as the cat decided to open those golden eyes and stretch his claws. 'Try me,' Reid told the formerly sleeping feline. 'I dare you to use those on me. Make my day.'

Cats were smart. Fluffy-Wuffy merely rolled to a sitting position and began to wash his face. 'What does playing trucks involve?'

'We find an empty truck and get in and pretend to drive. You can give me a proper driving lesson if you want,' his niece declared with a winning smile.

'You're *nine*.'

'And I can almost reach the clutch.'

'Piper, what did I tell you about not bothering Uncle Reid?' A new voice had joined the throng, but Bridie didn't venture any further than the doorway.

'You said never wake a sleeping tiger but he was *awake*. And he'd kidnapped Fluffy-*Wuffy*!'

'Lies. All lies,' he mumbled in protest. 'By all means, take the cat.'

'I've just had a call from Ari,' Bridie said. 'She mentioned she'd been trying to reach you.'

'Uh-huh. I've been asleep.'

'Her contract terms state that someone needs to do a final inspection of site six and sign off on it. I've done the first five. You want to take this last one? You could organise a pilot and get up to the site this afternoon. She tells me this one is the crew's favourite. Her favourite too. She's incredibly talented. Her outdoor spaces are such sensory escapes.'

'Then tell her we'll waive the inspection clause and sign off on it and she can be on her way.' A pillow hit him in the head and sent an unexpected jolt of adrenalin through his system. 'Hey, mind the skull!'

'Tell her yourself. Get up.' It was Bridie as he'd never heard her before. 'Piper, take the cat to the kitchen and give him some food. And stay downstairs until I return, okay?'

Surprisingly, her daughter did what she was told.

Reid warily sat up and put the pillow behind him, out of easy reach. 'Something you want to say?' He'd never been at the pointy end of Bridie's displeasure before. He didn't like it.

'Yes, I have something to say. I've been wanting to say it for a while. Stop sulking around feeling sorry for yourself. Get up, get active, and go and sign off in person on the job *you* set up, and give the woman *you* pursued some kind of praise and closure when it comes to the enormous project she took on for *you*.'

Ouch.

But he did have decent arguments to present in his defence. 'One: Ari has benefitted from my patronage, and I don't owe her anything,' he declared coolly.

'And two: I don't see how it's any of your business to tell me how to run *my* business.' Never mind that those lodges were half hers and they were in business *together*.

Bridie glared at him. 'I say this with love in my heart for you, Reid, but you're being an arse.'

'Playboy, remember? Not a good bet when it comes to women wanting anything more than a quick once-over. I saw, I conquered, I'm done.' Surely that load of steaming excrement erupting from his mouth would get Bridie gone?

His sister-in-law merely tossed her hair behind her shoulders and crossed her arms. 'Bull.'

'You've just never seen my playboy ways up close.'

'If you mean I've never seen you happier than when I went to collect you from Ari's work site five weeks ago, then no. I've never seen that before. And then you pass out on a rock face and decide you're no good to anyone—which is blatantly untrue—and ghost the woman you're in love with and who is in love with you! So, you tell me…what's going on?'

'She's not in love with me. I was a means to an end, nothing more. It's fine. She's fine.'

'I'm not buying it, Reid. You care for Ari more than you're letting on. I can see it in you. You're letting good things go because of a minor…physical…' she waved a hand towards him '…glitch.'

'Does this pep talk have a point?'

'Yes, and I've made it. Get out there and engage with Ari. Sign off on her work. Tell her it's genius, because it is.'

'I said I'd sign off on the job and I will.'

'And *don't* leave her hanging on a personal front,' said Bridie. 'You're better than that. I don't care what playboy hat you think you're wearing. One way or another, clear the air.'

'The air is clear.' He'd scorched the earth while he was there, but surely the air had cleared. He was letting Ari go for her own good!

'Good.'

'Are we done?'

Bridie hovered uncertainly. 'I do love you, you know. I don't think you're useless or unworthy or whatever's going on in your head. So there are things you can't do any more. So what? Reorient towards what you can do.'

So they weren't done… 'Bridie, you've had your say and I love you for it. I've heard you out. And I think I've taken advantage of your hospitality for quite long enough. I'll be on my way home within the hour.'

'Which home?'

'Cooper's Crossing.'

Her eyes narrowed. 'There's no one else there.'

Reid smiled mirthlessly. 'Exactly.'

An hour later, an anxious little girl stood in front of the screen door that would lead Reid to the waiting helicopter and pilot. He had his carryall in hand and his wraparound sunglasses in place and did he not look like an uncle who was going somewhere?

Whoever said the blocking of one sense would stimulate other senses knew what they were talking about. He'd added another sense since his eyesight had dimmed. He now had the unwanted ability to read other people's body language.

He refused to call it reading someone's emotional aura.

'Are you coming back tomorrow?' Piper asked.

'No.'

Agitated arm swinging ensued. How did a person keep a child they adored at arm's length? 'But I'll be back.'

'Will you be you again?'

What a question. 'I might be a little bit new. But people always change. You'll have changed a lot by the time you grow up, and even after that. We all do.'

'But I can still love you, even when you're new,' the little princess said. 'You don't have to teach me how to drive, you know. We can do other things together that are fun.'

'You're right.'

'I can read to you.' She shuffled from one foot to another, her anxiety spiking his. 'If you like.'

He hated the very thought. 'I'd like that.' There he went again, lying to a loved one. 'And I'm learning to sing. You could have lessons too.'

Shoot him. Shoot him now. 'I could.'

'Do you want to take Fluffy-Wuffy home with you for company?'

He'd found his line in the sand. 'No!' Hell, no! 'Thanks, Pip, but no. He'd miss you too much.'

'Not if he had you.'

How he got out of that house without crumbling in a heap, he never knew.

'Take me to the eco lodges at site six,' he said to Judah's new helicopter pilot who'd been brought on six months ago after it had been made clear to all that Reid's days of being a flying taxi service had come to an abrupt end. The man was more than competent and, beyond a nod and a gruff, 'sure thing' didn't feel the need to fill the air with conversation.

So what if Reid didn't have his hand on the joystick of the helicopter as it ate up the ground between Jeddah Creek and Cooper's Crossing? He could still appreciate a blue sky all around him and the feeling of going somewhere. He had red dirt below him and a work site to inspect and a part of him relished having something concrete to be responsible for. He wasn't completely useless. If all else failed, he could while away the hours by torturing his nearest and dearest with his singing. Maybe he really did just need to re-examine his priorities in the face of this latest health setback and set a new course and get on with it. Maybe Bridie *had* managed to pillow-slap a little sense into him after all.

He was even looking forward to being in Ari's garden space. It wasn't as if she would be there. He'd checked with Bridie, who said Ari was hundreds of kilometres east, working on another job.

He'd texted Ari in reply to her missed message and said he was inspecting site six today and ex-

pected to sign off on it later this evening. She'd
sent him a single line in reply.

Thank you for the opportunity to shine.

An hour or so later, the pilot set the little aircraft down a short distance from the new landscaping, and they waited until all was still before
getting out and securing the blades.

'Not sure how long I'll be,' said Reid.

'I brought some paperwork with me.'

'Use one of the cabins if you like. I'll find you.'

They set off together towards the trio of buildings. Of all the sites where the lodges had been
built, site six was by far his favourite. It had been
built on the curve of a permanent water channel and huge river redgums dominated the landscape to the southwest. Even with his limited
eyesight, he could appreciate the pale glow of
the tree trunks and branches when the late afternoon sun hit them just right. Tendrils of the
mighty Diamantina river cut the floodplains to
the west, bringing birds and wildlife close.

Before Ari, a couple of waddi trees and random
mounds of saltbush had dotted the area between
the three cabins, and basic walking tracks had
been stomped into place between one cabin and
the next. The cabins had provided refuge from
the heat of the day or the winds that whipped

dust into every crevice and there had been little
reason for anyone to gather outside, but now...

While the pilot headed for the nearest cabin,
Reid turned left and followed the circular dirt
track surrounding all the buildings—its edges
now defined by scrubby acacia trees and flowering understory plants he'd only ever seen during a big wet.

Ari had ringed the entire garden area with
thick Corten steel posts planted close enough
together to let small creatures in and the hun-
griest herbivores out.

He turned inwards and crossed a narrow walking bridge over a shy, trickling stream filled with
rocks and grasses and alive with the sound of
frogs and other insects. Snakes and lizards too,
he'd bet, although he didn't see any.

Ari's answer to that had been that there would
always be snakes in paradise and that the balance
of nature demanded it. She'd assured him she'd
made every effort to keep people on the walking tracks and had made the outdoor gathering
areas as uncluttered as possible, with no spots for
creatures to hide without being seen.

She'd kept the waddi trees and the circle theme
and added paving and places to sit, and curved
shelters, half wall half roof, that provided various levels of shade. There was a sunken fire pit.
A viewing deck with a curved back wall and not

one but two porcelain bathtubs open to the sky and sunset views, with a rustic wooden table sitting between them.

The ground beneath the tubs was some kind of smooth concrete mix set with tumbled stones and pebbles from a riverbed. They'd been laid out in snakelike curves, and he remembered from her notes that the idea was for people to walk on them barefoot and massage their feet while their bath was filling up.

Reid turned on the taps to one of the tubs and let the warm, clear water run through his fingers as he stared at the outline of his favourite river redgum in the distance. He could smell eucalyptus and a fainter scent of something sweeter. He heard the buzz of insects nearby, but they seemed to have other things to do than bother him.

The water reticulation overhaul Ari and her team had given this place was genius, cobbled from a research paper outlining ways in which the Israeli desert had been turned over to food production, and a regional zoo's schematics for a closed water system that grew endangered turtle species.

The whole set-up for growing plants and redefining habitat here was ambitious, possibly foolhardy, and he anticipated no shortage of scientific minds wanting to track the system's progress for years to come.

He didn't notice her presence at first.

He hadn't heard her approach over the splash of the water into the bathtub. But he sensed something, maybe just the stirring of the air, and when he turned, there she was, leaning against the wall, silently watching him. She wore cut-off shorts, a short-sleeved yellow top, and work boots and she looked relaxed and not at all surprised to see him.

He, on the other hand, was extremely surprised to see her. Glad too, if the sudden leap of his heart before it settled into rapid drumming was any indication. He wished, more than anything, that he could see her face and the expression in her eyes. Then again, if he could still do that, he wouldn't have turned her away in the first place. He would have still had enough to offer her. 'This is unexpected.'

'Bridie told me you were on your way here, and I was in the neighbourhood so here I am.'

'Trespassing.'

She put her hands in the pockets of her shorts and nodded agreeably. 'Again.'

He loved the sound of her voice and the ease with which she navigated uncertainty. He relished her dry wit and sheer practicality when it came to traversing this Outback landscape. She belonged here, more than anyone he'd ever met.

Her spirit called to his.

He'd never been so tongue-tied or so fanciful.

'What do you think?' she asked. 'I have a morning tour, a midday tour and a sunset tour all planned out.'

'It's half past five.'

'I know,' she replied dryly. 'You will be difficult and turn up in the in between. But even if you don't want the tour I can stand here and tell you that I planted the area around this bathing ledge with tea trees with antiseptic properties, and wattle that helps with aches and pains, and she oaks whose cones are said to help with rheumatism. In times to come you'll be able to pick a posy and add it to your bathwater. The aloe in the pot over there is good for sunburn, you probably know that already. Gert has a recipe for a cream. I thought it might be fun to make up a batch and leave it in the cabins, along with the recipe, but that's overstepping my brief by a few hundred kilometres or more. That sweet smell is brown boronia. I found a guy who'd been grafting it onto different root stocks, so I went a bit mad and planted hundreds of them.'

He could listen to her talk about plants until the end of time. Maybe he'd imprinted on that particular pastime in the tent. 'Will they live?'

'So far so good.'

'I had my workshop engineers read your water schematics out loud to me. They added supersized whiteboard visuals and that helped. They're fans of your work now. So am I.'

'Thank you. I've been tweaking the water reticulation systems all the way along but this was the first time I had a permanent water supply to dip into. I think it went to my head.'

'The results speak for themselves.'

'I'd really love a maintenance contract that covered an entire year, but I guess putting something together and then handing it over to others to care for is all part of the business.'

'It's going well? The business?' So stilted and formal, but he didn't know how to be anything else without reaching for her.

'Very well. I've been getting more enquiries than I know what to do with. I feel like I'm on a runaway road train. I'm sure as hell not the one driving it.'

He'd felt that way too, early on in his career. Of course, he hadn't admitted it quite as readily. She would need good people around her for guidance and support. He could—

No.

He could step back and let her soar.

'Been slaying any demons lately?' she asked lightly, but it wasn't a careless question. She was signalling a move from business conversation to the personal.

'None. You?'

'I'm employing my younger brother as a full-time labourer—he's a hard worker, it's going well. And I've been to a barbecue at my father's place with all his family present. They were all terrifyingly friendly, even the pregnant dachshund. I may have said yes to one of the puppies. I'm not entirely sure what I said, to be honest. Fear of rejection brings on the crazy talk in me. Like now, for example.'

'Did you tackle your stepfather as well?'

She shook her head. 'Too risky. He's too deep in the bottle right now. That's not my fight.'

'Wise.'

'I have a healthy sense of self preservation. Unlike some.'

He deserved that.

'Do you ever wish we could go back to the tent and just talk?' she asked quietly. 'Because I've been wishing that a lot. Whatever else, we were honest about our needs back then. We wore our vulnerability with ease.'

'It was memorable.' On that he could agree.

'I keep wondering what I'd say or do to let you know how much I respect and treasure you.' He stilled and she drew a quick breath and kept right on speaking. 'I'm crazy in love with you, but I might have forgotten to mention it last time we spoke. I wondered whether you'd missed that about me, what with your no longer excellent eyesight. I mean, do you really need to see me light up like Sydney Harbour bridge on cracker night whenever I see you?'

He wanted to see that so badly.

'You should ask my crew about the way I behaved the day I found out you'd been in that cliff accident. So much stomping around and staring tragically at my phone in between trying to call you. I already knew you were smart and generous and could make me feel good about simply being me, but that was the day I realised how much I wanted to have the *right* to be there for you.'

'You want someone to need you, that's all. And I refuse to be your patient.' Finally, some spoken words he actually *meant*.

'I've thought about that.' She crossed her arms in front of her, classic defensive posture. 'Another demon I wrestled with while I tossed up whether to track you down again or not, because I do like being needed, yeah. Trying to fix you while you were hurt made me feel that I had something of value to offer. And afterwards, you went out of your way to make me feel good about simply being me. You made me believe I had plenty to give, so here I am. Making my play for your love and attention. Again. Just in case I didn't give you enough information the first time.'

She took a deep breath—he could hear the inhale even if he couldn't see her chest rise with the effort. 'I can't make you love me if you don't—it would be foolish to try. But if you're pulling away because some of your body parts don't work the way they used to and you no longer believe that what you have to offer is enough, just *stop* with that way of thinking.'

She unlocked her arms and spread them wide as if offering him her all. 'Your dodgy eyesight isn't going to keep you down for long. It isn't going to prevent you from loving someone with all that you are. There are so many ways to connect. A million ways to show and feel love. What's one more curve to navigate? That's what I really came all this way here to say. If this is the end of us, I didn't want to finish it by being cranky with you. You deserve better than that. I can *be* better than that.'

'You're going to go a long way, Ari Cohen.'

'Maybe so.' She tapped her heart. 'But this? For better or for worse, this is yours. And you know where to find me, if ever you want to get in touch.'

'May I kiss you goodbye?' His words came out all cracked and torn.

She took a step back. 'Best not. I'll cry.'

He closed his eyes and turned away.

And she was gone.

CHAPTER FIFTEEN

AFTER ONE WEEK of solitude, Reid was second-guessing his decision to let Ari walk away. After two weeks, he'd taken to living in one of the cabins at site six and walking the tracks she'd laid out for him several times a day. In the mornings he listened for the birdsong. At midday he sought out the shady rest areas. Come sunset, he could be found in a bath, watching the colours of romance and fire light up the sky.

He found a carved wooden walking stick hanging from a tree branch on one of his walks. Oiled and knotted and handy should he ever encounter a snake he wanted to send on its way without getting too close.

He found an ice pack for migraine sufferers that covered a person's forehead and eyes in every freezer in every cabin.

He found a single lens binocular, a monocular, in the bird hide that had been built in the curve of the channel bank and used it to bring the moon close enough to see every colour with his one good eye, with its pinpoint tunnel vision.

His phone did not stop ringing, with his key employees asking for his opinion on one thing or another, and he came slowly to the realisation that he wasn't superfluous to requirements and his brain worked as well as it always had. He was a linchpin in a world he'd spent many years building and that wasn't about to change because his vision was no longer twenty-twenty.

Demons were being slayed. Time was taking care of them.

Time and the slow realisation that he was still capable and needed.

Ari's landscape worked its magic on him and brought him back to his senses, and those senses were stronger now, stepping up, getting a work-out here in this garden of sensory engagement.

Ari was like no one else he'd ever experienced.

It would be his pride and his pleasure to walk through life with her, and she was right there, waiting for him to catch up and recognise what she already knew.

Happiness was spending a lifetime with someone you loved and who loved you right back, no matter what the limitations or challenges ahead.

The day he discovered the tiny Matchbox car racetrack hidden beneath a sprawling salt-bush—with tunnels and cars parked in finger-made caves—and it took him straight back to Ari as a child, and the challenges she'd faced and the way she'd created worlds using nothing but wonder and imagination—he knew that letting her go was going to be impossible.

He loved her.

He needed her.

He wanted her, and every adventure that came of it.

Beyond belief.

Reid sat at the outdoor table between three cabins, the visit from his brother and sister-in-law not exactly going to plan. His medical records lay spread out in front of them, and Judah, for one, was relishing every bit of being a big brother hell-bent on making the most of his little brother's discomfort.

'Tell me again what we're looking for?' Judah asked silkily.

'Anything I might need to explain in detail to someone who...' *loves me* '...might want to be with me romantically. A future wife, for example.' He refused to be embarrassed. His question was legitimate. If he was going to track Ari down and lay his medical future out before her and beg her forgiveness for ever turning her away, he wanted a second opinion on what information to include.

Would he lead with his healthy sperm count, for example? Or the metal in his head that still needed to come out? Or a comprehensive explanation—or demonstration—of the limits of his eyesight?

'Start with your eyesight,' said Bridie. 'It's a lot worse than I thought.' Worry laced her voice and she reached for his hand and threaded her fingers through his. 'I'm cross you didn't tell us how bad it was.'

'I thought it'd improve.' His defence was three-fold. 'I didn't want to worry you. And I didn't want anyone to fuss.'

'Tell me again how Ari came to you and told you none of this matters and you turned her away,' murmured Judah.

'She should have tied you up and convinced you,' said Bridie firmly and Judah just about snorted his coffee.

Dearie me, was there a story there that Reid could use to throw a little shade Judah's way? Could something useful come out of Reid's hasty decision to call in the troops to help him plan his offensive on Ari's emotions? She deserved a grand gesture, and he was working on it. 'What was that, big brother? You agree?'

But Judah recovered fast, his momentary splutter replaced by steely composure. 'And *after* coming clean about your eyesight, and future changes to it, you might want to mention your artificial hip, missing spleen and the not so insignificant repairs they had to do to the artery in your groin. You could finish with this little gem from your team of specialists. *"Mr Blake's speedy recovery has been nothing short of miraculous."'* Judah's curt voice effectively conveyed his displeasure, no need for Reid to see the finer details of the other man's scowl in order to get the message. 'Why didn't you *tell* us?'

'We all had a lot going on and I didn't want—'

No one jumped in to put words to Reid's thoughts. 'I didn't want to appear weak in front of you. That was why it hit so hard when I went climbing and came unstuck and photos of my unconscious self being lowered to the ground by a bunch of helpful strangers got splashed across social media for all to see. There it was. My frailty exposed for all to see.' Reid appealed to his brother who'd spent over seven years in prison being a badass so that other inmates left him alone. 'Judah, you *know* there are times when a man can't be seen to be *weak.*'

Judah ran a frustrated hand through his hair and looked to Bridie, who huffed and threw up her hands. 'He needs us. This is very clear.'

'Do you think grovelling should come before the facts or after the facts?' Reid asked, gesturing with his hands towards his medical records.

'Before.' Bridie sounded very, very sure.

'Not even sure you need the facts,' Judah murmured.

'I need you to help me craft an email regarding my ongoing health challenges,' Reid told them. 'That's step one. And I want your thoughts on step two, which is seeing her again.' He didn't want to fail Ari again. Never, ever again.

His beloved sister-in-law sent him a wide, sunshiny smile that he'd long since learned to associate with outrageous ideas. 'I have an idea.'

CHAPTER SIXTEEN

WHEN ARI HAD received Reid's email, with a dozen attachments containing medical records and a brief explanation that this was why he'd tried to end their relationship, she hadn't known quite what to think.

The brief had been brutally matter-of-fact and his medical records had been stomach-churning. He'd had a far harsher time of it than he'd ever let on. He'd be grateful if she took the time to consider the information and get a good notion of what choosing to love someone like him would mean for her future, should they decide to embark on one together. Full disclosure was obviously needed, he'd written, in order for her to make a fully informed, rational decision.

Definitely an engineer, she thought. Since when was love rational?

He'd finished the email 'Reid'.

Below that, though, had been a treasure trove of words.

Your Reid.

She liked that one.
It had been followed by:

What if she doesn't reply? How long should I give her before I call? I should say, 'I'll call in a couple of days'. Or, no, too needy. I should ask her to call if she needs more information—write that down. 'Call if you need more information.' Or, no. Just my signature will do. Just Reid.

Dammit, Judah, why are you grinning? What do you mean, how can I tell? You have a mouthful of teeth as big as a corn cob and whiter than the moon. I can see them! Yes, I will practise my poetry before I see her next, you tool. Just help me write the goddamn letter.
Respectfully Reid?
What do you mean too many Rs? I always sign my letters 'Respectfully'.
Who in the world uses the word 'felicitations'?
You call this helping?
Just finish it and press send!
Your Reid.
Felicitations, Judah.

Ari had read that spiel at the end a hundred times over and it still made her grin like a woman with a corncob mouth. It gave her the confidence to wait a day and fully digest the information in those attachments before replying.

Dear Reid,
    This explains a lot, although not quite everything. Your brother is awesome, btw. Would you like to meet to discuss mutual future prospects? I'm crazy busy prepping for my next job at Black Ridge, but I'm free on Saturday.
    Your Ari

When an email reply came through for her with an invitation to meet him at Jeddah Creek station homestead at four p.m. and prepare to stay for dinner and that she was welcome to use Gert's old room if she'd like to stay the night, Ari agreed to everything. He was obviously back at his brother's place for a while and there were more than enough rooms for them to speak privately.

She definitely wanted another look at that bonkers family library.

Saturday morning brought a phone message from Bridie, saying she was sending a helicopter for Ari to save her the bother of driving.

Ari had been back at Gert's by then, dropping Jack off, before getting back on the road.

She didn't say no.

When Ari saw that the field next to the homestead was full of light aircraft, luxury jets, and
Outback vehicles and tents of every kind, she
turned to her taciturn young bush pilot. 'What's
going on down there?'

'It's for the ball.'

'Ball?'

'Spring Fling charity ball for rural health services? Ring any bells?'

Not one bell was being rung. 'And it's on…
tonight?'

'Starts at six p.m.'

'Oh.' Bridie had neglected to mention it. Last
time a ball had taken place here, Ari had been
staff. 'Fancy that.'

It was hot, dry and dusty in the aircraft parking lot. People were bringing out the sisal mats
and fairy lights and setting up their luxury and
not so luxurious camping spots. Piper was sitting on the steps, a little grey cat lounging regally
beside her. The girl jumped up and waved to her
enthusiastically. 'Mum, she's here!'

And then Bridie appeared, dressed in a sleeveless yellow cotton frock and enough sparkly jewellery on her fingers and wrists to make it clear
that the mistress of the house was dressing to
impress. Her hair was up and make-up expertly
applied and made the most of her flawless features. Ari felt altogether plain in reply. 'You're

just in time.' Bridie hugged her, and since when were they on hugging terms? 'The stylist has just finished my hair and you can slot in next.'

'Um, Bridie? Hello. Thank you for sending the helicopter to collect me, and I can see you're really busy, and I'm pretty sure I missed a memo because I had no idea this was a ball weekend, but if you need a hand—'

'No! No hands. All will become clear in time. Come in. Please. I have a gown for you, I had to guess your measurements, it came in this morning, and if you don't like it, we'll raid my closets.'

'A…gown.'

'*Very* modern-day ballroom elegance. Valentino. Full confession, I *did* help with the selection. Reid paid.'

'Where *is* Reid?'

'He was with Judah earlier, but I've lost track of them. We don't need them yet.'

Bridie gave Ari no time to protest as she led her into a beautifully appointed guest bedroom set up with two beauty stations. 'Ladies, this is Ari. Ari, this is Darla, magician hair stylist, and Casey, make-up artist extraordinaire. They're here to help. And this is your gown, and a few pairs of shoes to choose from—I wasn't sure how high, but I do remember you wore heels when you were here before, so I didn't stint.'

Ari stared in wonder at the gown displayed on

the headless mannequin in the corner. It was a deep, dusky blue festival of froth, shot through with gold and silver meteor streaks originating from one side of the seriously tiny waist. It was strapless at the top, the chiffon skirt caressing the ground. It was the most elegantly romantic confection she'd ever seen. 'That's for *me*?' she squeaked.

'Do you like it?'

How was that even a question? 'I don't understand.'

'Reid wanted you to have the full Cinderella experience. Apparently, he owes you one.'

'He doesn't.'

'Ah, well. Work it out between you,' Bridie said blithely. 'We have two hours before we have to be ready, and I still need to see to a few details before I have to become Lady Blake of the Outback for our overseas relatives.'

'You have overseas relatives attending too? Fancy relatives?' Ari had barely got her head around being friendly with Reid's regular billionaire and altogether famous family members.

'A very special one,' confirmed Bridie. 'Reid doesn't know yet, but Judah's been corresponding with her for weeks.' Bridie's smile broke as she leaned in close to whisper in Ari's ear, 'We found the missing sister. And she's magnificent.'

Wide-eyed, Ari stared at the other woman with dawning delight. 'Really?'

'Yes. But it's a secret. This night is full of them so zip lip, buckle up and enjoy the ride. Are you with me?'

'Yes!' Abandoning all objections, Ari spread her arms wide and let happiness take hold. Although, hands. Hands that had been scrabbling around in the dirt all week. 'My nails belong on a troll.'

Casey held up a packet of something and rustled it gently. 'Got you covered, sweetie.'

'We good?' Again, Bridie left no room for argument. 'Yes, you've got this. Enjoy. See you soon.'

It was what Ari had always imagined getting ready to be married would be like. The fussing and the primping. The detailed discussions about smoky eyes versus dewy innocence. Given that stunning gown in the corner, Ari's hair would of course be styled up. Audrey Hepburn in *Breakfast at Tiffany's* got a mention and they ran with it. Ari had not a scrap of jewellery to complete the look, but that dress was its own shining star and didn't need any accompaniment.

By the time they were finished with her, and Ari stood staring at her reflection in front of a wall full of floor-to-ceiling mirrors, her transformation was complete.

Ari Cohen was no more.

This person was someone new, and Ari couldn't wait to take her for a turn in the ballroom.

'How does it feel?' asked a voice from the doorway, and there stood Reid in full black-tie regalia.

'Excuse us,' said Ari's magic helpers and Reid smiled at them as they slipped past him and out of the room.

'It feels like a fairy tale,' she told him. 'I will never trash the Cinderella experience again. I'm a believer. Although...' It was probably time to come clean. 'You know how I can't actually swim?'

'Mm hmm.' He sounded dreadfully indulgent.

'I can't waltz either.'

He laughed at that, and she flung herself into his welcoming arms, and he held her tight and buried his face in her neck. She could feel his ragged breaths against her skin and the rapid tattoo of his heart against her chest. 'Missed you, Ari,' he murmured. 'You wouldn't believe how much.'

'I might believe it.' She'd worked her fingers to the bone hoping that exhaustion would stop her from missing him. 'I missed you just as much.'

She breathed out a sigh at the solid, all-encompassing strength of his embrace. 'I want whatever future you're imagining for us. I don't care what it is, I just want to be there for it. With you.'

'I want everything you have to give.' He released her and stepped back and reached into his pocket and brought out a small velvet box. 'This was my great-grandmother's. I had it sent from England. You're going to love England when we finally get there. So many gardens.'

He opened the box and held it out to her with both hands. 'I'd get down on one knee but I'd need a cane to get back up, or you could heave me up but that's not the effect that I'm going for. I'm vain enough to want to camouflage my failings, but I hope to hell I'm smart enough to hold onto the best thing that ever happened to me. I won't ever turn you away again. I will be there for us. I'll show up and do the communication work needed to offset the things I cannot see. I will never let you doubt my love for you. I'll wear it out loud and it'll be there for all to see.'

He looked into her eyes and she could have sworn he saw clear through to her soul. 'Ari Cohen, I love you. Will you do me the honour of spending your life with me, marrying me, being with me for all the turns and twists ahead? I can't promise a smooth and easy road, but I can promise that I will love, honour, and cherish you for as long as I draw breath.'

'Yes.' She sought his lips with hers and fed him love, make-up ruined by the tears in her eyes and the fierce tenderness of his lips. 'Let's do that, yes.'

Drinks flowed, music played, and the ballroom was full of people who'd dressed up and turned up to get a little Outback dust on their heels, admire a tangerine sunset that stretched on for ever, and enjoy an evening of outrageously opulent Blake hospitality.

Ari's diamond engagement ring glittered in the lamplight as Reid introduced her to friends and business partners, rescue workers and support staff with the ease of a born people person.

No one could tell the extent of his injuries hidden beneath his expensive designer suit. No one had any inkling of the emotional journey he'd undertaken and the changes that had been wrought.

Strong man, to have recovered from such injuries.

Smart man, to have confronted his insecurities and examined them and laid them bare for his loved ones to see.

Her man.

'You're glowing,' he murmured, leaning into her for a moment before straightening again.

'Lit up like the Thames on New Year's Eve.'

'Have you ever been to London on New Year's Eve?'

'No.'

'We're going.'

No objections were forthcoming. Ari's world was ever expanding, beyond her imagination, and she was ready for it. With Reid in her arms and his love to keep her safe, she was ready for whatever the future held for them. And then a willowy blonde woman walked up to them and commanded attention.

Was this the super special guest? It must be.

'Reid Blake? Please allow me to introduce myself.' She had a charming English accent. Crisp. Aristocratic. Wary rather than warm. 'My name is Victoria Colby-Jones. *Lady* Victoria Colby-Jones. Your brother found me, after some rather unorthodox digging.'

Reid's expression swung from shock, to disbelief, punctured by a couple of rolls of amazement, before he finally settled on a kind of kid-under-a-Christmas-tree delight. 'Vic! You even look like me, I can tell. Only female, and shorter.'

Lady Victoria's generous mouth firmed. 'Quite.'

'Look, Ari. It's Vic!' Ari wondered whether an elbow to the ribs would dampen his joy. 'Vic, this is my future wife, Ari.'

Lady Victoria looked her up and down and finally pronounced judgment. 'The pleasure is mine. Is Ari one of those hideous Australian nicknames and your given name is Ariel?'

'No. I'm just Ari.'

'Ah.'

Judah and Bridie joined them and formed a tight circle. Reid was quick to commandeer his brother.

'Does she need a hug? Does she look receptive to hugging?'

Judah leaned closer to his brother, but his eyes didn't leave his newfound half-sister's face. She could hear every word and everyone in the small standing circle knew it. 'No.'

'Got it,' said Reid as Ari took the opportunity to grind her stiletto heel into the toe of his gleaming leather shoe. 'Darling, mind the toes,' said Reid at his most injured. His thousand-watt smile brightened as he returned his attention to the newcomer. 'Lady Victoria, do you waltz, by any chance?'

'Of course I waltz, Ree…'

Everyone waited for the end of Reid's name to drop. It didn't.

'May I call you Ree?' his half-sister asked in dulcet tones. 'I'm doing my very best to fit in and failing miserably, I can tell.'

Ari's estimation of the haughty lady rose exponentially. 'Have you seen the sunset yet?' she asked.

'Vulgar,' Lady Victoria proclaimed. 'And yet somehow captivating.'

Bridie lured a hovering waiter forward and rescued three champagnes from a sparkling silver tray. One for Ari, one for Lady Vic. The other one she drained.

'Lady Victoria. Sister,' said Reid at his warmest. 'Have you ever tried to *teach* a woman to dance in the middle of a crowded ballroom?'

'No.'

'Would you like to?'

'No. I far prefer to make a fool of myself and other people in private.'

Which was how, at the end of a beyond perfect evening, Ari found herself in clearing ringed by ancient stones, beneath a giant redgum tree, barefoot in the dust in a Valentino dress, and with a couple of strings of fairy lights and a waxing moon to guide her way. Five people. Two brothers, a newfound sister, and the women those brothers had chosen to love.

And no one else to witness them making a spectacle of themselves.

They'd been learning how to waltz beneath Victoria's steely gaze. Swapping partners. Learning how to touch and to move together in acceptable ways. Someone to lead and not always the male partner. Someone to follow. Give and take and perfect moments of togetherness to be found in there somewhere.

'Waltzing is respect wrapped in gossamer,' Victoria declared. 'It's intimacy tempered by society. Waltzing properly with someone you love is perfection.'

Ari and Reid found their perfection as they shuffled closer and simply held each other close. 'Is she real?' asked Ari.

'I think so, but I'm exhausted,' murmured Reid. 'If I don't lie down soon I'll fall down and I've done quite enough of that lately.'

Ari had an idea but she didn't know if it would fly. Not in these clothes, but the stars were right there, millions of them in an inky sky. 'Do you trust me?'

'For ever and beyond.'

She was doing this. Stepping out of Reid's arms, she raised her hands in a bid for attention and took control. 'All right, people. Line up. Lady Victoria in the middle, Reid and Judah on either side, Bridie, you're next to Judah on that end, and I'm here next to Ree. Now hold hands.'

'Is this a dance?' asked Lady Victoria suspiciously.

'Kind of. It's a soul dance. It's how Reid and I first met, and it's an ice breaker. Hold hands, please, and lie down.'

'You mean in the *dirt*?' Lady Victoria wanted clarification.

'Yep. Right here. Right now.'

'But our gowns will be *ruined*.'

'But you'll see the stars like you've never seen them before and feel the weight of your body pressing into the earth and you'll get to say hello to this place in a way you'll never forget.' She took Reid's hand. 'They're just clothes. Beautiful clothes, granted, but they've done their job this evening, haven't they? They're just clothes now.'

Ari couldn't make anyone comply with her wishes. The men weren't moving. Everyone was waiting on Lady V.

And then, with a dancer's grace, Lady Victoria sat down and everyone else followed. Bridie laughed. Judah snickered. Reid cursed, and then they were all on their backs in the dirt and it was visceral and magical for those who knew how to lie back and close their eyes and feel.

Ari felt Reid's hand tighten around hers. Silence had never been more serene.

'Welcome to the family, Victoria,' Judah said gruffly. 'We might not be what you're used to but there's love for you here if you want it and beauty and truth and openness beyond imagining.'

Victoria was silent and time seemed to stop as everyone waited for her reply. Would she want what they were offering?

'Thank you, Judah, and Reid, and Bridie and Ari. Thank you so much for your hospitality and welcome.' Her voice cracked on that last word. 'I want it.'

EPILOGUE

IT WAS A wedding small and intimate, with red dirt at people's feet and brilliant blue sky overhead. Gert was there as auntie of the bride, wearing a burnt-umber-coloured silk dress and hat that she and Ari had shopped for together. Bridie and Piper were matron of honour and young bridesmaid, stunning in deep ivory silk with red and orange accents. Ari's stepbrother Jake was there, wearing his first ever suit that he'd begun saving for as soon as he'd received his invite. He'd turned into a startlingly handsome young man and he stood quietly beside Gert and winked as Ari passed them by. Judah had been pressed into service as Reid's best man and stood strong and firm next to his brother.

And then there was Reid, his wild curls almost but not quite tamed and the eyepatch over his left eye giving him a rakish air that he did his very best to live up to. While the sight in one eye had faded, the other eye had strengthened.

With that one bright hazel eye in play, he still saw more than most.

He thought her beautiful, even when she was up to her elbows and knees in dirt and surrounded by flies, and he told her so every day, using his words and his gaze and in a dozen other tiny ways.

It was in the cup of tea he placed at her elbow on the early mornings when he had to attend one of his numerous business meetings.

It was the way he closed his eyes and drew her into his embrace just to breathe in her scent.

It was in his touch when, finally, she stood in front of him in her wedding finery and he reached for her hand.

She'd chosen to wear a simple white sheath of a wedding dress with off-the-shoulder sleeves and a tiny waist. No veil, no gloves. She carried a wedding bouquet of all her favourite native flowers. Flowering gum and flannel flowers. Lamb's ear and banksia cradles.

She wore her hair loose and her make-up was flawless courtesy of Bridie, who'd helped her dress.

On her bedside table this morning, Reid had left a long velvet box and in it was a diamond bracelet that matched her engagement ring. Something old, his note had said. Her something borrowed was a handful of delicate opal hairpins that Bridie expertly slid into place after twining several strands of Ari's hair into an elaborate flower shape above one of Ari's ears. Her something new and blue had come from Gert—a gossamer-thin wrap of sky-blue silk to drape across her back and over her arms and dance with the afternoon breeze.

Piper stepped forward to take her bouquet and Reid immediately reached out to capture that hand too, a smile breaking over his handsome face as he studied her.

'Your eyes are telling me you love me,' he murmured. 'Best day ever.'

'I've words of love for you too, so you can remember them in the dark.'

'Perfect.' He leaned forward and pressed his lips to her cheek. 'You're absolutely perfect for me. I have so many words of love for you too. Want to hear them?'

Happiness bloomed, strong and sure. This beautiful life and this brilliant, loving man were hers, and she would cherish them from this moment forward.

'You know I do.'

* * * * *